Dear Rea

They say March comes in like a lion, and on a blustery day, there's nothing better than four sizzling Bouquet romances to warm you from head to toe.

Legendary, award-winning author Leigh Greenwood sets the pace this month with **Love on the Run,** as a woman desperate to clear her name discovers that the P.I. hired to help her may be a danger himself—to her heart. In **Little White Lies,** from favorite Harlequin and Loveswept author Judy Gill, a contented bachelor who needs a fiancée for a month only learns that his "intended" is the one woman he could love forever.

When two stubborn people collide, it's a sure thing that sparks will fly. In Harlequin author Valerie Kirkwood's **Looking for Perfection,** a small Kentucky town is the setting for a story about two single parents who find love in a surprising place. Finally, Silhouette author Mary Schramski takes us on a search for **The Last True Cowboy,** the story of a hard-living rodeo rider—and the woman who's stolen his renegade heart.

So curl up with your favorite quilt, a cup of tea, four breathtaking, brand-new Bouquet romances and dream of spring!

Kate Duffy
Editorial Director

TWO MINDS, ONE HEART

"Your ranch meant a lot to you, Trace," Beth said. "You and I are the same in that way."

"The same?"

"Wanting a home. In other ways, too. We both had marriages that didn't work, and we're both determined not to get involved again."

Trace Barlow really did want a home, a place to feel he belonged. All his words about being a tumbleweed were just words—maybe even a way of protecting himself.

"Beth, I think you know me too well." Trace whispered her name just the way she liked to hear it.

She nodded. "Yes, maybe I do." God, she was falling in love with Trace, and there wasn't anything she could do about it.

Without another word, he seized her wrist and brought it to his chest. Beth could see the need in his eyes. She wanted so much to be a part of him.

As if he could read her mind, his arms wrapped around her, and he brought her close. They kissed as if they'd kissed a thousand times before.

A few dizzy moments later, Trace cradled her easily in his arms, his lips against her ear.

"Where?" was all he said, yet she knew exactly what he was asking. . . .

THE
LAST TRUE
COWBOY

MARY SCHRAMSKI

Zebra Books
Kensington Publishing Corp.

http://www.zebrabooks.com

This book is for Amanda Simmons,
Janey Casey and all the other great
mentors in the world. Thank you.

ZEBRA BOOKS are published by

Kensington Publishing Corp.
850 Third Avenue
New York, NY 10022

Zebra and the Z logo Reg. U.S. Pat. & TM Off.

First Printing: March, 2000
10 9 8 7 6 5 4 3 2 1

Printed in the United States of America

ONE

Trace Barlow stood in the middle of Branding's small, quiet courtroom and regretted doing ninety on his way back from Abilene. He'd gone there to check out the new rodeo arena, got to talking to a couple of the guys about the competition, and let the time get away from him.

Now he was standing in front of Branding's only judge. He'd seen that expression before on Carol Kelly's face. She was mad as a rattler being poked with a stick.

"Trace, darn it." Carol's eyes narrowed. With a resounding thud, her gavel connected with the judge's bench. "Aren't cowboys afraid of anything?" Crows'-feet gathered and feathered back to her graying temples.

Trace scraped his fingers through his hair. "You know the answer to that one. I was trying to get back to Branding early so I could get in some practice time before dark."

Carol shook her head. "Driving that pickup like you're coming out of the chute?"

"That same day I found out I'm losing the lease on the land—"

"You still have to follow the law—"

"And the Abilene rodeo's coming—"

"Save your breath, Trace. I've heard every excuse in the world."

Carol's cheeks were red, and Trace knew he'd pushed his luck. She shot him another familiar glare. They'd known each other for years. Hell, when his mama had taken off, his daddy had enlisted Carol's baby-sitting services.

"I'm giving you fifty hours of community service. I know hitting you in that empty wallet won't work, but I'm not going to stand by and watch you and every other cowboy in Branding kill themselves in souped-up pickups because they've got rodeos coming up."

What in tarnation is she talking about?

"Community service? How about just a lecture about my evil ways?" Trace smiled when he knew he shouldn't. Just because he and Carol went back a ways didn't mean she wasn't a serious judge.

"I believe I've given you that lecture. Even though you don't care about your safety, I do. Take a look at your busted-up leg. Ever think you're getting too old to compete in rodeos?" Carol arched her brows.

"Twenty-nine is not too old for roping." Trace filled his lungs with cool air. Someone had opened all three windows, and a late spring breeze whispered through the room. He didn't need to be reminded a Brahma had stomped on his leg in a few places. When a hard rain drenched the north Texas town, the deep ache in his bones and the limp was enough of a reminder.

Trace studied Carol again. By her expression, she wasn't about to budge, so he might as well get it over with. "OK, what the hel—heck is my sentence? Picking up litter on Beautify Branding Day?"

Carol shook her head. "I'm modernizing this courtroom. Mentoring is the way of the future." She shuffled through some papers, then held up a single sheet. "Here it is. New folks, just moved out from Dallas. Boy is in a tad of trouble and on probation." She glanced at Trace for a long moment, then continued. "He's ten. The Dallas County caseworker recommended a mentor, a role model."

"I'm no *role model.*" Trace's chest tightened and he clenched his jaw. He wasn't cut out to be any kid's hero.

The bang of her gavel echoed through the room. "I'm not asking you to be a hero, just talk to the child. The family lives out at Oak Creek Ranch, off Jessup Road. Spend at least ten hours a week with him until you do fifty hours."

"Carol, have a heart. I don't know what to say to a kid. Besides, I've got to find land for my cattle till I can buy back my ranch." He hadn't been around kids much. With ranching and practice, he wasn't around anybody much.

"Talk to him about life . . . how no one should break the law."

Trace snatched his cowboy hat off the table, settled it on his head, then shifted the brim to the right. He glared at Carol from under the black felt. The woman could be a piece of work. His dad had always said she was the *hardheadedest* person he'd ever met.

"Take off that hat in my courtroom, or you'll be doing sixty hours."

"Thought you were finished." He removed the hat.

Carol put the paper down, and her gaze softened. "Trace, this kid needs help from someone like you. You know right from wrong. He'll sense that. Just spend some time with him."

"I've got plenty of work—"

"I know this last year's been hard for you. You might find mentoring interesting."

Carol's gaze hardened, and he knew changing her mind was hopeless.

"Then again, Carol, maybe not."

The faded sign at the edge of the highway announced Oak Creek Ranch. Trace downshifted and slowed to make the sharp right. The long gravel road curved left, then made a soft right turn that led to a white clapboard house sitting on a grassy patch of land.

Trace rubbed his chin. Last he heard, an old man from Houston had bought Oak Creek. He looked east and drank in the sharp sunshine inching its way across the flat blue sky.

At six this morning, he'd prowled one pasture and made mental notes of what fences needed mending. Then he'd practiced roping for an hour before driving out here.

He'd decided two hours ago he'd spend thirty minutes max with the kid. Then he'd head back to his fence fixing, ride the rest of the pastures, and get some more practice in.

A moment later Trace pulled up in front of the ranch house and let his pickup idle. The front shades in the sash windows were up, but the place looked deserted.

What in heck am I doing here?

He didn't have any business talking to a kid who couldn't keep his butt out of a jam. What did he know about kids? He had enough trouble keeping his own life straight.

Trace shut off the truck. As he climbed out of the cab, the front door opened and a face pressed against the screen.

"M-o-o-o-m."

Trace chuckled in spite of his bad mood. In some ways, boys never changed. The kid, a shock of blond hair hanging over his forehead, opened the screen door and walked out onto the wrap-around porch. The door whacked against the doorjamb as the boy took the three porch steps all at once, his blond hair flapping against his forehead, his face pinched into a sullen stare.

Trace leaned against the fender of his pickup and hooked his thumbs in his pockets.

"You from the court?" the kid yelled across the yard.

Close up, he looked younger than he had on the porch. His eyes were wide, a little fear hidden behind them. He was as gangly as Trace remembered being at that age—all arms and legs.

"Trace Barlow's the name. Are you Ben?" He extended his hand, but the boy ignored it and just nodded.

"Mom told me about you yesterday. How'd you get stuck with me?" He hitched his thumbs in the pockets of his shorts and angled his arms the same way Trace had. A sad look clouded his large blue eyes.

"Wouldn't call it stuck. Where's your parents?"

"Mom's in the kitchen. And, boy, is she in a bad mood."

Trace rubbed his chin with his thumb and forefinger.

Nice way to start my morning, with some mama upset about her baby boy being in trouble.

"Your mama in a bad mood a lot?"

"Mosta the time." Ben kicked at the dusty gravel. "Ever since we moved out to this dumb one-horse town, she's been pretty hard to live with."

Trace's own mother had been long gone by the time he'd reached Ben's age, and his old man was hardly ever around.

"She's not happy 'bout you, either." The boy poked his finger at Trace.

"Yeah?"

"Said at least five times she's known enough cowboys to last her three lives." Ben jammed his hands deeper into his pockets.

"Guess she doesn't like cowboys." Trace hitched his thumb under the brim of his cowboy hat and shoved it back a little. That was all the conversation he had in him for any kid. He'd never gotten used to chitchatting.

Shifting his gaze eastward, Trace let the cool morning breeze dance against his face. The squeak of the screen door brought his attention back around. He squinted, trying to focus his eyes against the bright sun.

A vision of a woman, as pretty as he'd ever seen, floated down the steps. She appeared delicate but strong, sexy but wholesome. She walked toward him with purpose in her step.

She had blond hair like the boy, and she'd pulled it into a ponytail. Translucent tendrils of hair fluttered around her oval face. As she drew closer, the sunlight created a white-gold circle of pure light around her. She looked unreal—like an angel.

Trace blinked.

A half second later she stood in front of him, her hands on her shapely hips. She'd tucked a simple white T-shirt into loose-fitting blue shorts, and her feet were sheathed in ankle socks and tennis shoes.

The kid turned toward her and frowned. Her expression softened when she looked at Ben.

Trace nodded a hello.

She smiled at him for a quick moment, then drew her attention back to her son. "Ben, your breakfast's ready." Her hand went to the thick shock of hair that hung over the kid's forehead, and she pushed it out of his eyes.

"Mom." Ben stepped away from her and shook his head. His hair flopped into his eyes again. Without another word he turned, and stomped across the dusty yard, up the stairs, and slammed the screen door.

Trace turned back to Ben's mother. Her attention was still on Ben. Wisps of hair brushed against her high forehead. Thick eyelashes accented large eyes that were the same translucent blue as the morning sky. Light freckles graced her high cheekbones, and her mouth, even in profile, was full, her bottom lip lush and soft.

An unfamiliar feeling rolled up Trace's spine. He sucked in air and tried to bury the sensation.

"I'm Beth Morris." She smoothed the tendrils of hair back, but in a moment, they danced against her cheek again. She held out her hand and Trace shook it.

Her skin was as cool as he imagined. Despite his dry mouth, he introduced himself.

"Judge Kelly called me yesterday. Thank you for driving all the way out here. I apologize for my son's manners." Her gaze drifted back to the ranch house, and she sighed.

"No problem." Trace couldn't take his eyes off her. On the gravel drive, Beth Morris stood out like the only Texas wildflower in a dusty field.

She faced him again. Her eyes weren't just one shade of blue. They were light and dark and in-between. Just looking into them reminded Trace of the way he felt when he won a rodeo competition.

Her tongue darted out and wet her bottom lip.

The question of what it would be like to feel her moist mouth on his do-si-doed through his thoughts.

Keep your mind on business, Barlow. The thought brought him back.

"I know the court thinks Ben needs a mentor, but I don't think he does," she said.

Her words reminded Trace of the reason he'd come out to Oak Creek Ranch in the first place.

"I don't know much about this mentoring thing. Haven't been around many kids," he said.

"I tried to talk the judge out of making Ben participate in the program, but she wouldn't hear of it."

"Carol's pretty hard to convince when she's got her mind made up." Trace tried to shift his gaze to something else, but he couldn't stop staring at Beth.

Her blue eyes widened. "You know Judge Kelly?"

"Yep. We've both lived in Branding all our lives." Trace pushed his hat back a little more.

"The judge is coming out tonight to talk to Ben and me about the mentoring program. I'm going to make her see I can handle my son just fine without any help." She crossed her arms.

Trace's attention drifted to her pretty mouth again. Her lips were bare and the same color as some roses he'd seen once.

He didn't need to be thinking this way about a woman like this. He had enough problems. Besides, he didn't want any trouble from a mad-as-a-hornet husband.

"Your husband doesn't like the program, either?" He definitely needed a wake-up call.

Beth's eyes narrowed a little. "I'm not married."

"Just you and your son out here?"

She nodded. "As I was saying, I don't think my son needs a mentor. I'm dealing with him just fine. Judge Kelly wants to meet Ben, so I thought that would be a good time to tell her again, try to make her see this situation won't work."

All Trace could think of was kissing her pretty lips, but Beth Morris had *nice* written all over her.

"I know Judge Kelly thinks Ben could use a man's influence, but I'm working hard to be both parents." She paused, pressed her full lips together, and stared at the ground. Then suddenly her blue gaze pinned him. "I might as well be truthful. I don't think it's a good idea for anyone who's involved with the rodeo to be around my son."

Beth Morris was not only good-looking, but honest—a lethal combination, in Trace's opinion.

"Ben already told me you think cowboys pretty much stink. And since I don't know much about this mentoring thing, seems like none of us should be put in this situation."

For the first time in a long time Beth felt her cheeks color in embarrassment.

Ben and his preteen honesty.

Well, she couldn't fault her only child for telling the truth. She *had*, in a fit of disbelief when the judge told her whom she'd chosen as Ben's mentor, said out loud, over and over, she didn't need any cowboys interfering.

And Trace Barlow was definitely a cowboy. His faded black hat announced he was used to being in the hot Texas sun.

Her gaze drifted to below the brim he'd pushed back. Black brows that matched his hair underlined a wide forehead. His eyes, brown as Texas earth, were almond-shaped and sun lines etched his face.

With his masculine nose and thin-cut lips, Trace Barlow could be on a poster representing Texas cowboys. That hard yet sexy look gushed out of him like oil from a Texas rig.

Her stomach tightened.

She glanced down at his hands.

They were cowboy hands, large, tanned, and callused from plenty of use. Just like Ray's. Hands that could make a woman feel out of control— but they just happened to belong to men who rode animals that bucked their riders senseless, cowboys who took big chances and left families. America's rodeo heros.

She bit her bottom lip hard.

Ben didn't need to be mentored by this man. Her son had already asked too many questions about cowboys, rodeos, and competitions. She wasn't about to let Ben start thinking he could compete in any rodeo event.

They'd been through tough times before, and they'd get through this one. She wanted to watch her son grow up and live for a long time, and she wasn't going to give up on that dream now.

"Looks like we've got one mighty big problem on our hands," Trace said, his tone deep and secure.

Beth shifted her gaze to his. "I'm sorry my son was so honest, but it's better you find out now."

"No problem. Always like to know where I stand."

For some silly reason, Trace's deep voice made her remember last night, when she'd found time to pour herself a glass of iced tea, sit on the porch, and stare for a few moments at the dark sky littered with stars.

Those few, fleeting minutes had been the first

time in months she'd forgotten about their problems and been able to relax.

She connected with Trace's gaze again. He was still staring at her. Goodness, his eyes were brown. For an instant, she wanted to know more about the man. Beth cleared her throat. She was being silly. She shouldn't care what this man was about, and the idea of his being Ben's mentor was even sillier. She could take care of her son just fine—*alone.*

"Since we both feel the same way, the judge will have to change her mind," Beth said, as much to get her mind off Trace and his dark brown eyes as to reassure herself.

For a quick moment she glanced at the clapboard house, hoping to settle the uneasiness dancing inside her.

Trace cocked his hat back more. "I'd really like to get out of this mess, too, but I think you need to know a little more about Carol before you try to goat rope her into changing her mind."

TWO

"Do you mind if we move away from the house? I don't want Ben to hear any of this," Beth said.

Her son had been upset when she'd told him they were moving to Branding. And when she'd told him the judge wanted to assign him a mentor, Ben had sulked for hours.

Trace nodded and they walked across the stiff buffalo grass. Beth noticed right away that Trace Barlow walked with a slight limp. Her heart pounded into her throat. Rodeo cowboys always thought they were invincible. Hadn't Ray thought so, too? Maybe she'd made the wrong decision about moving to Branding. It wasn't going to be easy keeping Ben away from people who loved the rodeo.

She pushed back the thought, telling herself she'd made the right choice. A big city wasn't the place to raise a rebelling son. Branding and her father's ranch were much better for Ben.

After crossing the front lawn and rounding the porch, Beth and Trace headed to a large live oak fifty feet from the house. Long ago, someone had placed a rough bench underneath it.

Beth sat and pressed her palms against the weathered wood. Trace took off his cowboy hat. The band had plastered his hair against his forehead. With a practiced hand, he smoothed the thick brown thatch off his face and then looked at Beth.

"How are you planning on changing the judge's mind?" he asked.

The man was certainly direct.

"Well, I'm just going to talk to her. She'll see my point."

"Carol's pretty much of a hardhead."

Beth couldn't help but laugh. "I'm sure she'd be flattered to hear your opinion."

Trace chuckled and shook his head. "She knows what I think and knows it's true."

Beth's chest tightened. The judge had to change her mind. She couldn't let Ben be influenced by anyone who lived and breathed rodeos.

"When she comes out this evening, I'm going to make her see my son doesn't need you," she said, and then regretted her blunt words. But it was true. Ben didn't need to hear about Trace Barlow's rodeo adventures. Her son was thinking too much about it as it was.

Trace glanced back to the house. "Does Ben's dad live around here?"

Beth stared at him. She couldn't help but notice how Trace's shoulders stretched his simple plaid cowboy shirt to its maximum. It also covered his flat stomach and narrow waist.

"He passed away." Beth shifted. Marking her husband's death with three little words always felt so uncomfortable. Ray had been too young, too alive. Those three words were old people's epitaphs.

Ray Morris had seemed bigger than death—laughing, talking, winning everything he set out to, until the night in Fort Worth when his luck changed and he'd been killed while bull riding.

"Sorry to hear that," Trace said, his voice low. "Must be tough for your son, too."

"That was nine years ago. Ben doesn't remember much."

Trace nodded and stared at the ground. Mourning doves cooed and called to each other before he spoke again.

"Mind if I ask what the kid did? Carol didn't tell me."

Since she'd moved out to the ranch her father had left her, Beth hadn't talked to anyone except the judge about Ben. For some reason, a little part of her wanted someone to be interested in her son.

"He snuck out and tagged with a group of boys." A lock of hair tickled the side of her face and she brushed at it.

"Tagged?" Trace's dark brow arched toward his hairline.

Beth rubbed her wet palms against her shorts. Even now it made her nervous to think of her son out in the middle of the night, running down a deserted Dallas street. "Kids get cans of spray paint and write words and symbols on buildings. It happens so much in Dallas, I take it for granted everyone knows the term." She stood and gestured toward the bench. "Please, sit down."

"Nah, rather stand. I rode all morning. Feels good to stretch my legs." Trace shifted his weight a little, then squinted as if pushing back pain.

Beth remained standing. She'd seen Ray put up his guard like that a thousand times—ignoring aches and sprains, even the pain of broken bones. He'd never wanted to acknowledge the rodeo might have beaten him a little. She'd always thought if Ray had acknowledged the danger, the golden rodeo light he'd managed to stand in might not have been worth all the suffering.

Trace tore a leaf from the tree and studied it. "Come to think of it, I have heard of this tagging on the news. Sounds like a prank. Most boys get involved with playing practical jokes. I did. Hell, I drove the town sheriff crazy when I was younger."

"Tagging goes beyond practical jokes, and a lot of kids who tag are in gangs." Beth looked at the house. It was still hard to believe Ben had done what he'd done. She shifted her attention back to Trace.

He was still watching her with his dark gaze.

For some reason, butterflies began to flutter in her chest.

"Gangs," Trace said. "That's not good at all." He hung his hat on a short tree branch above them, then tilted his chin a little and gazed up at the sky through the lacy patch of leaves.

Trace was at least a head taller than she, and Beth could see three fading lines—scars—on the underside of his jaw. Ray had called his many scars badges of courage. Yet to her they symbolized recklessness, the reason Ben hadn't had a father even when Ray was alive.

"What did you do?" Beth asked, then wished she hadn't. It didn't matter what crime the man had committed. He was not going to mentor Ben if she had anything to say about it.

"Ma'am?" His dark brown gaze was on her again.

"Why the community service? Judge Kelly didn't go into details." The turmoil in Beth's chest increased. She fought the uncomfortable feelings. The move and Ben's problems were stressing her out. Just yesterday, when Ben had smarted off to her like every other kid in the world did, she'd dropped a carton of eggs and broken all of them, then started crying like a baby.

"I was driving too fast. Carol's trying to cut down on the speeders in town." Trace's lips parted and formed a crooked grin.

Beth relaxed a little.

"I'm not a serial killer. Don't think Carol would let me off so easy."

His chuckle made her feel like smiling when she didn't want to. "That's nice to know."

"Not many criminals in Branding. You've only been here a few weeks?"

Beth nodded. Two weeks ago, with a big knot in her stomach and wondering if she was doing the right thing for Ben, she'd packed up the car with their belongings.

"You moved all the way out to Branding for your son when you don't have much use for cowboys and rodeos?"

His voice was laced with concern, something she hadn't heard in a long time, and it made the odd feeling in her body increase.

"I had to get Ben out of the city. I can keep him away from rodeos." When the juvenile authorities had visited and told her Ben would be on probation, the decision to move to her father's ranch was easy to make.

"Nice to meet someone who cares about their kid, but this is a big spread for a city woman." Trace glanced toward the pasture.

"I lived in small towns when I was growing up. Besides, my father died and left it to me."

"I don't remember seeing you in town, *ever.*" His brow arched a little, telling her he would remember if he'd noticed her walking down Branding's dusty sidewalk. That made her feel good.

"I've never been to Branding before. My parents were divorced and my mom moved around a lot."

"Your dad owned the ranch and you never came to visit?" Trace's eyes narrowed.

"I lost touch with my father a long time ago." She'd idolized her dad so much when she was a little girl. Then one day he'd just disappeared, leaving her and her mother to fend for themselves. That was the first time she'd learned people she loved too much could fade away like yesterday's sunshine. She'd never seen him again until it was too late.

Trace's gaze narrowed a little more and he cocked his head toward her. "That's too bad."

"I'm doing just fine." And Ben would be OK, too, as soon as their lives straightened out and she could convince her son he didn't need the rodeos the way his father had.

"Planning on cattle ranching? This is prime grazing land."

Beth laughed at his suggestion and brushed away the hair tickling her cheek.

"Even though I lived in small towns before Dallas, I don't know anything about ranching. I wish I did. It might be a way to put food on the table," she said, although there was no reason to share her problems with a stranger.

Beth stared down at the grassy spot in front of her feet. From what she could tell by the paperwork she'd been going through in her dad's desk, cattle ranching had been his intention. Thank God Oak Creek was free and clear.

"I'm no stranger to money problems either," Trace said in a low voice.

Beth didn't have to look up to know Trace was still looking at her with his darned concerned brown eyes.

"I'll find a way. I worked as an office manager in Dallas." She hooked her gaze with his. Yes, there it was—that look of concern.

She laughed nervously, and her attention slipped to his hands, to the tips of his fingers so easily hitched in his pockets. Yet she could see the calluses on the edges from rodeo practicing. "Don't worry. Ben and I'll be fine. I'm very good at what I do."

"I bet." His thick brows lifted, and a mapping of lines from too much sun wedged across his forehead. "Thing is, there aren't many offices to manage around Branding."

"Ben and I will get along just fine. We always have." She took a step back. All she wanted right now was to be left to raise her son and figure out what she was going to do in a few weeks when her money ran out.

Trace knew he shouldn't ask so many questions, but he couldn't help himself. A troubled look had inched its way into Beth's pretty blue eyes and made his chest tighten.

She straightened a little like a cat who'd just been awakened from a nap. It was easy to see she was a mighty proud and independent woman.

"I *hope* Branding and the ranch will be a safe place for Ben."

"This town's a good place for kids to grow up." Branding had been good to him, even after his old man had run off. People had pitched in and helped him and encouraged him when he'd won rodeo events. They even threw him a party one time when he'd finaled in Fort Worth.

"I've already told Ben he can't get involved in any rodeos. It's too dangerous."

"Rodeo helped me grow up." Trace shifted his attention toward town. Beth's worried gaze did make him wonder, for a split second, how he'd handle the problem if he had a son who needed help.

Hell, he couldn't even hold a marriage together. How in tarnation would he be able to handle a kid in trouble?

He looked back to Beth. Her lips were pressed together in a worried line, but they still looked soft and sweet. A tiny leaf from the live oak had fallen and found a home on her shoulder. His fingers tingled with the need to brush it away. Trace reached out and touched the spot. The leaf floated to the ground.

Her body heat wove its way through her thin cotton T-shirt and found his fingertips.

Beth pulled back slightly, her eyes questioning him.

"A leaf was on your shirt."

Her brows knitted and a tiny wrinkle formed between them. "You can leave now. I promise I'll get you out of mentoring my son."

In the pearly morning light, Beth seemed vulnerable, and Trace's stomach clenched. She didn't look old enough to have a kid Ben's age, and it was clear she didn't know what she'd be facing with Carol.

She took a step back and gazed at him. "I wonder why the judge thinks you'd make a good mentor for Ben?"

Trace laughed. Obviously she was thinking out loud. "Yeah, I wondered that, too."

Beth blinked and laughed nervously.

The sound, fresh and sweet, made Trace feel confused. The cool morning breeze danced against his hot skin.

"I'm sorry. That wasn't very thoughtful." Her chin dipped a little and she studied the ground again. "I'm sure you're wonderful with kids. I was just . . . I don't want Ben influenced by anyone who has anything to do with rodeos."

"No problem."

"Besides, you and Ben don't have anything in common."

"We've both been in trouble with the law. I've got a lead foot, and he likes to paint other people's property." He couldn't resist the tease. Beth was trying not to smile but lost the battle. She looked up at him, a grin gracing her lips.

"Ben's an artist, and he's very good. He loves to paint."

Trace wanted to hear her laugh again. "So do I. Just finished painting the fence around the house I've been renting—"

She giggled, and his chest tightened with attraction for the woman standing in front of him.

"Ben's won art awards. He's the most talented child. Teachers have told me they've never seen anyone his age . . ." She shook her head and her ponytail bounced. "Geez, I bet I sound like a bragging mom."

"You sound like the right kind of mama. I don't blame you for being proud."

For a quick moment, Trace wondered how soft her skin would feel against his fingers, yet he knew he didn't need to be thinking about feminine dimples or brushing his fingers against sexy shoulders.

She kept smiling, and his heart crashed against his rib cage. The need to take Beth into his arms rolled over him like a Mac truck.

Damn! He should be practicing his roping or looking for a new place to graze his cattle, not standing under a shade tree talking to the prettiest woman he'd ever seen.

Trace cleared his throat. "I still don't think you're gonna talk Carol out of her decision."

Beth's soft blue-eyed gaze dropped to his hands and quickly shifted back to his face. "I won't have Ben influenced by cowboys, rodeo people."

"Most rodeo people are nice folks." Hell, the rodeo had saved his life when he was younger, put food on the table, and made him feel like he was someone. It still did. This morning when he'd thought about winning the Abilene competition, he'd felt on top of the world.

Her slender fingers clenched into fists. "I'm sure you've had a different experience than I have. I'm trying to keep my son safe."

Beth Morris was interested in her child, and he didn't know anything about kids or what made a good family. Hell, he'd never had much of a family. His bum leg sent a sharp pain to his hip. He shifted, then watched as her fists unfurled.

"You're right. I don't know anything about kids, family," he said.

"Well then, it's settled. You won't mentor Ben. I'll tell the judge you backed out. She won't have a choice. She'll have to rescind."

Trace's chest tightened. Carol would throw his butt in jail if he didn't comply with her court order. "Wait a darned minute. I'm not backing out. Just tell her you don't want me."

"I've told her that, and she wouldn't listen. The only way out of this is to tell her you won't do it."

"I don't plan on spending the night in jail if Carol gets her tail in a twist." He ran his fingers through his hair. It was common knowledge Carol got madder than a bull with a bee sting when anyone went against her court.

"She has to change her mind." Beth's gaze filled with determination. She was spunky. Trace liked that in women, but he wasn't going to jail for anybody.

The morning breeze picked up her scent and brought it to him. He couldn't help but think of warm Texas nights and clean sheets. His stomach clenched in an unfamiliar way.

Beth cleared her throat. "Just go on home, and I'll explain to the judge you didn't feel you were the right person for—"

"No way."

"Pardon me?" Her pink tongue slipped out to moisten her lips.

"Carol will have my hide, and I don't have time for that. Abilene rodeo's coming up. I'm practicing a lot." Trace took a step forward, close enough to notice the tiny flecks of dark blue embedded in Beth's eyes.

"Of course, your rodeo is more important."

"Yeah, it's pretty important to me." Trace raked his fingers through his hair again. He didn't even know this woman, and she was confusing him. "We both agree I shouldn't mentor, but telling Carol I've skipped out isn't going to work. She'll just increase the hours—or worse."

Beth looked up at him. "Why, I wouldn't think you'd be afraid of some small-town judge." She straightened her shoulders and looked more than pretty.

She was nudging him, teasing him. Trace took a step back and reminded himself he didn't need to get all riled up about Beth Morris.

"Beth, I'm talking common sense, not fear. Jail

isn't my idea of a good time. Besides, my three hundred head of cattle don't take care of themselves."

"She might throw *you* in jail?" Her delicate blond brow arched as if taking flight and her lips curved into a smile.

"Yeah, and *you,* too."

"Me?" A shapely hand fluttered to her heart.

"Sure, she's got quite a reputation. Surprised you haven't heard about it." Trace couldn't help but laugh when astonishment grew in her eyes.

The woman was as cute as a bug in a rug.

"Really? I hadn't heard." Beth's mouth formed a worried yet pretty pout.

"Yeah, she doesn't put up with any bull when it comes to her court orders."

Beth flopped on the bench and sighed. Then she turned toward him, her eyes still wide, her mouth parted.

They stared at each other for a long moment, and Trace's blood raced through his veins.

"I can't go to jail. What in the world would Ben think? And I've got to look for a job."

"Let's use some common sense. We both agree this mentor thing won't work." He spoke to calm his body down, more than anything.

She nodded.

Trace continued. "Best thing is to follow her court order today, show her we tried. Then, when you talk to her—"

"Me alone?" Beth's eyes opened wider. "Maybe we could do it together. I mean, present a united front and all that. You do know her. Will you come back tonight?"

Hell!

Now that she'd asked, he couldn't let her talk to Carol alone. "I guess I could—"

"Yes, we'll just explain you aren't right for Ben."

"And Ben doesn't like me," Trace added.

"I'm sure he won't." She nodded.

"We got along just fine out in the drive," Trace said and motioned back to the house. The kid seemed to be all right with him.

"I'm sorry, I didn't mean to be rude. I'm sure you're a very nice man, but . . ." The little line between her brows appeared again.

"Don't worry about it. What time's Carol coming out here?" Beth was only trying to protect her kid, and he thought more of her for it.

"Seven, after din—"

"M-o-o-o-m!"

Trace and Beth turned. Ben was galloping across the yard toward them.

"So you'll come back tonight?" Beth stood, her arms crossed, the worried look still on her face.

He put on his hat. "Yeah, I'll be here. But I should talk to the boy just so we can tell Carol we tried and it didn't work."

Beth bobbed her head emphatically. "Yes, good idea—for a few minutes, anyway. Tonight we'll get the problem straight."

"Get what straight?" Ben asked as he bounded up to them, dust swirling around his ankles.

"Mr. Barlow is going to spend some time with you this morning. Did you eat all your cereal and take your vitamin?"

He nodded, then eyed them. "You've been out here talking for a long time. What's up?"

Beth straightened Ben's collar.

"Geez, Mom, leave me alone." Ben ducked his head and scuffed his right foot against the crisp grass.

Trace bet those words had been said a million times by kids all over the country. But when he saw Beth's facial muscles tense, he couldn't help but speak.

"That's what mamas are for—straightening collars and making sure you eat all your cereal."

Beth laughed, and the delightful sound stole Trace's rational thoughts again.

"Whatcha mean?" Ben asked, his face puckering in a frown.

"Your mama is suppose to hound you. Someday you'll be glad she did. That's what makes men out of boys." Trace wasn't sure how he knew this. His mother hadn't taken any interest in mothering him.

"I don't think so," Ben announced.

"Want to show me your ranch?" Trace asked. He needed to make a stab at being Ben's mentor so Carol could see he was all wrong for the job. To his surprise, Ben's eyes lighted up.

"Sure. See ya, Mom."

* * *

Beth watched her son walk away with Trace Barlow. Ben barely came to Trace's shoulder, but she knew in a few years he'd be as tall as the man walking beside him.

Although she'd found out Trace was pure cowboy, he didn't have the larger-than-life aura Ben's daddy had. Ray Morris had been spectacular looking, and he'd had a way about him—a ladies' man strut. Anywhere he went, a wave of attention surrounded him, and it got worse as his star rose in the rodeo circuit.

Beth pressed her lips together. She didn't need to be thinking about Ben's dad or all the bad memories that went along with him. For the two years they'd been married, she'd spent too many lonely hours worrying whether Ray would come home in one piece.

Her throat burned with all the jumbled thoughts. Seeing Ben with Trace brought the reality of her son's never having had the chance to know his father to the surface of her raw nerves. She swallowed hard and stared up at the blue, almost white-hot sky.

If it was the last thing she did, she was going to make up for all Ben had lost when Ray died. She'd keep her son safe.

Beth shifted her attention back to the twosome cutting across the field. Ben almost had to run to keep up with Trace's stiff-legged gait.

How had Trace gotten his injury?

The question startled her, and Beth chastised herself for even caring. How did any of them get hurt? Asking their bodies to do things they shouldn't, that's how.

She studied her son, who was running alongside Trace. They were headed toward the broken-down fence in the north pasture by the barn. She visored her eyes. Ben was wearing his red shirt—the one she'd bought him at the Dallas Art Museum.

Lord, how I love him.

Beth turned and crossed the lawn to the house that didn't seem like a home. She still had plenty of boxes to unpack, plus the chore of sifting through her father's possessions.

This afternoon she and Ben could drive into Branding and buy a paper. Maybe she'd find a job. She nibbled her bottom lip. A job in town meant she'd have to leave Ben longer than she wanted to. Her chest felt heavy and her temples pounded.

Beth took a deep breath. Now wasn't the time to worry. Their problems would straighten out. She opened the screen door and reminded herself the first thing on her list had to be talking the judge into changing her mind about Trace.

THREE

"Do you limp 'cause somebody beat you up?"

"Son, I don't get in many fights." Although surprised at Ben's remark, Trace couldn't help but laugh. He'd acted tough, too, when he was Ben's age and had said things he shouldn't.

"You must be a chicken. A real live 'fraidy cat. Men fight all the time." Ben curled his hands into fists and ran in front of him, yelling.

The kid was trying to show him how tough he was. Trace stopped and waited for Ben to turn and face him. "Let me tell you something. Don't say anything you can't back up, or you might be the one getting your butt in a jam."

"Well, I just meant . . ." Ben's gaze dropped for the grassy edge of the path.

Trace knew he shouldn't be giving the kid any advice, but Ben was the kind of boy who might shoot off his mouth to the wrong person.

"Ben, most men who put on a tough show aren't tough at all. To be a man, you've got to know you can handle any situation, and the way to do that is to use your brain." Trace curled his fingers into a loose fist and tapped his temple. "Brain power is better than fighting any day."

Ben stared at him, his mouth ajar. "Yeah, right! I'm not a sissy."

The kid was handling the world just as Trace had at that age—putting up a front for everyone, inside scared as hell. Trace could see the fear in his eyes.

"Ben, you need to think before you talk. Don't let your mouth get you in trouble." That same attitude had gotten him in plenty of jams.

"Think about what?" Ben asked, staring at him. The kid had his mother's eyes—innocent blue.

"Don't say something about someone unless it's important." Trace reached up and angled his hat, then turned back to Ben. "If someone is calling your mama names or hitting a girl, then that's something to stand up for."

Ben's eyes narrowed a little, like he was really interested, yet he didn't say a word.

Trace clenched his jaw. He had no business telling Ben about life. He didn't know anything about kids, and he certainly wasn't any kind of role model. He crossed the path to the run-down fence.

Ben ran to catch up. "How did you hurt your leg?"

"I went one way and a bull went the same way."

"You broke it?" Ben asked.

"Brahma did. In a few places." Trace's right

leg started to ache, and he rubbed his palm down his thigh.

"My dad's an NFR champion. He's the best bull rider in the world," Ben yelled out over the field.

Trace's jaw tightened more. Beth had said the kid's old man was dead, but Ben was talking like he was still alive. *Morris* . . . Years ago there'd been a Ray Morris who'd been a big champ, one hell of a star.

Trace looked at Ben. The boy was staring up at him, waiting for him to say something.

"Your old man's name Ray Morris?"

Ben nodded, a grin taking up much of the room on his face, his hair flopping into his eyes. "Yeah, the best bull rider in the world, maybe the universe."

Trace placed his foot on the first slat of the fence. The board gave way under the weight and split in two. He looked at the rest of the fence surrounding the pasture. It was old and in need of repair.

"Ray Morris is the best rodeo cowboy in the *world,*" Ben repeated.

"I've heard of him." Anyone who'd been involved in rodeos for any time would know the name. Ray Morris's record was still in the Rodeo Hall of Fame. Trace stared across the pasture. Morris had been a young hotshot, a golden boy in the circuit.

Trace pressed his memory hard. He'd heard talk that Ray Morris was a real party animal. Being a superstar, he would have gotten all the women and booze he wanted. A lot of young men had fallen into that trap.

"My dad was the best." Ben interrupted Trace's thoughts.

"He was a great bull rider." Trace looked down. So Beth had been married to Ray Morris. Trace's chest tightened. They had to have been kids when they were married.

"How many rodeos have you competed in?" Ben asked.

"A few."

"Still bull riding?"

"Nope. I'm roping now." He'd finally given in to the fact he'd never be a bull champ because of his leg, but he could still compete in roping.

Ben leaned against the fence like Trace. "Roping isn't anything compared to bull riding. You chicken?"

Trace turned to face the boy. "Ben, remember what I told you about thinking before shooting off your mouth?"

Ben kicked at the fence, but didn't say anything for a few moments. Then he spoke. "You like ropin' better?"

"Nope. Never wanted to rope, but with my leg busted up, roping's what's left to win any decent money." Trace drew in a chest full of moist air. He had it all planned. He was going to win the Abilene rodeo and buy back the ranch he'd lost because of his accident.

"My dad was the best bull rider in the world,"

Ben repeated with a smile on his face, yet his eyes held a world full of sadness.

"He was one of the best, that's for sure." Trace had dreamed about being an NFR champ long ago, but now he was satisfied with winning smaller rodeos, just being part of the excitement. Rodeos and the people in them were the family he'd never had. They made him feel he belonged, and he wasn't about to give them up.

"Yeah, *the* best," Ben said and stared out into the field. More hurt filled the kid's gaze.

Trace remembered what life felt like when the person you loved most in the world wasn't around.

"You miss your dad?" Trace forced the question. He wasn't much for talking about feelings, but for some reason he had to ask the kid.

Ben turned, his brows knitted. "My dad's dead."

"My dad's dead, too, but I miss him." A quick hitch in his chest caught him by surprise. It was the same kind of ache he'd felt at fifteen, when Luke Barlow drove out of Branding, and Trace had watched his truck disappear down Highway 45. That was the last time he'd seen his old man, yet he thought about him every day.

"I don't miss my dad." Ben jammed his hands in his pockets and his tough act appeared again. "I was only a baby. I'm almost grown now." The kid sniffed and rubbed at his nose.

Trace could tell he was hurting.

"I still miss my old man," Trace said. For some

reason he wanted to let the kid know it was OK to feel the way he was feeling.

"You do? You're an old man and you still miss your daddy?" Ben's eyes grew wide.

Trace laughed. At times his twenty-nine years felt plenty old. He looked at Ben. Hell, it wouldn't hurt him to be honest.

"Sure. It's OK to think about your dad. In fact, it's only right. You miss your old man all you want." His chest tightened more, and Trace took a deep breath to bury his own feelings.

Ben pushed back from the fence. "Still want to see the barn?"

"Yeah, if you're still interested in showing me." Trace glanced down at his watch. He'd stayed way over his time limit. Between fence mending and practice, he didn't have room enough in his life to swing a cat by its tail. But he made the mistake of looking down at Ben. The kid was waiting, excitement evident on his face. "But we gotta make it fast."

They walked toward the large, run-down barn, and Trace stared at the expanse of prime coastal grass blanketing the pasture in front of them.

His cattle would have a heyday with the lush grass that covered the earth as far as the eye could see. It was obvious the place had been used to raise cattle, but now it was dilapidated and in need of repair.

After they rounded the barn's corner, he spotted an open area in the ground. Trace cut away from Ben and crossed the ten feet. The ground well was uncovered. A moment later, Ben stood next to him, looking down the deep hole.

"I threw some pennies in there. Never heard them hit bottom, though."

"This old well is pretty dangerous sitting open like this. Anything around we could use as a cover?" Trace asked.

"There's wood in the barn."

Trace followed Ben and helped open the squeaky barn door.

"Will this work?" Ben pointed to the stacked wood.

The kid was smart and resourceful. "Yeah. Help me get it out there."

Ben ran to the pile.

"Just watch what you're picking up. Brown recluse spiders like to hide in places like this." Trace carefully picked a board out and checked both sides.

Ben mirrored Trace's actions, easily pulling out a piece of wood and checking it. Trace smiled. Not only was the kid smart, he learned fast, too.

After they covered the well, Trace wiped the dirt off his hands and Ben did the same. "Let's put this extra back and close up." They walked into the barn and restacked the planks. Trace gazed around the empty enclosure. "Nice barn."

"Mom let me put my artwork in the back." Ben stared at the cement floor and scuffed the toe of his tennis shoe against it.

"Want to show me?" Trace asked before he

thought about what he was saying. He needed to get back to work, to practice, to his own problems.

"Nah, you wouldn't be interested. You're a rodeo rider. It's just some stupid drawings I've done."

"Come on, I'd like to see them."

Ben opened the door to the small room in the back and flipped on the light. "I wanted the bigger room and bathroom upstairs, but Mom said no."

They stepped inside the room. On every wall, even on the cement floor, sat pictures. Images of cities, people, and cars shimmered and came to life in brilliant colors.

"Pretty stupid, huh?" Ben asked in a bored voice.

"You did all these?"

"Yep."

Trace crossed to the middle of the room. He didn't know anything about art, but anyone could see Ben had talent.

"Mom said I started drawing pictures with crayons when I was two. She's always talking about how she had to wash the walls and stuff."

"This looks mighty good." Trace leaned down and picked up a sketch of Beth. Ben had captured the beauty of her eyes perfectly. Trace's mouth grew dry. He tried not to stare, but couldn't help himself. "You draw this?"

"Yeah, from a picture I took out of our album.

It's not finished yet. I've got to paint it. Thought I'd give it to Mom for her birthday."

Trace stared at the image, and his chest hitched up more. He handed the picture back to Ben. "You've got talent, son."

"But painting and drawing, those things are for sissies. Rodeo isn't. In Dallas, kids called me names because I can draw. I'm going to be in the rodeo like my dad."

"Talent doesn't have anything to do with being a sissy. You should be proud."

"That's what Mom always says." His lips turned downward.

"Your mama cares about you."

"Mom doesn't understand that painting is for nerds and geeks."

"Those Dallas kids are jealous because you've got a talent they don't have. Look at that fifty-seven Chevy pickup over there. Now that's cool." Trace nodded toward the opposite wall. The chrome on the grill actually seemed to flash and wink.

"You think so?" Ben stepped back a little and stared at his work.

"Sure. You gotta believe in yourself, in what you're good at. Maybe you could draw something about cowboys. There's a lot of western artists." Trace racked his brain for the name of the artist who had made the cowboy statues he'd seen in Fort Worth when he was at the stock show.

"Really?" Ben glanced around the room. "I want my dad to be proud of me. I've gotta do something he would like—like bull riding. I know he'd want me to be just like him."

"I'm sure he'd be proud of your artwork. Any fool can bounce around on a horse, but this is good, real good." Trace reached out and patted Ben's shoulder, not sure what else to say to the kid. "We'd better get back. Your mom'll be worried."

Trace glanced at Beth's image again.

A flash of attraction jolted through him, and he gritted his teeth against it. It was best to stay away from women like Beth, but it would be a mighty long time before he forgot her pretty face.

"So, you coming back?" Ben asked when they were halfway to the house.

"I'll be here tonight to talk to the judge. Your mom and I think it's better someone else spends time with you. Someone who knows about kids."

A dark look flew into Ben's eyes. "You don't like me."

"You're just fine," Trace said evenly. The expression on the kid's face proved he wasn't a mentor.

"Yeah, right!" Ben yelled, then he took off across the field in a dead run for the house.

Trace's first thought was to chase after the kid, but then he ruled against it. It was better this way. Ben would get someone who knew what he was doing, and he'd have time to practice.

He found his pickup and opened the door. Before climbing into the cab, he looked back at the house and hoped for a minute Beth would come out.

He didn't need a sledgehammer to make him see the woman didn't want anything to do with him, but he still wanted to see her again. A moment later, as if he could wish it true, Beth's silhouette was framed in the front window.

Trace's stomach tightened. Beth arched her body, lifting her arm a little, and he saw the soft under-curve of her breast beneath the white T-shirt.

A strong jolt of attraction attacked him again. She was one good-looking woman.

Trace climbed in his truck and started it. His manhood tightened the crotch of his jeans. He shouldn't be thinking about Beth, a woman who looked like an angel but placed cowboys a peg below the devil.

He made a U-turn and traveled down the gravel drive. Tonight when he and Beth talked to Carol, things would get straightened out. Tomorrow Ben would have a person who knew how to help him, and Trace could get on with his life.

FOUR

Beth wiped her hands on the kitchen towel, picked up the folded newspaper, and headed out to the porch. Before she even opened the screen door, the cool evening breeze feathered against her warm skin.

She crossed the porch and stood at the top of the first step. Against the horizon a slash of black slid along the highway, slowed, and turned up the gravel road. Dust billowed around the truck as it plowed down the driveway, pebbles thumping against its large tires and hubcaps.

Beth glanced at her watch. It was only six-thirty. Trace Barlow was certainly punctual. Beth opened the paper to the small section of want ads and tried to study them, but she kept peeking over the edge of the newspaper. Trace pulled his truck in front of the house, opened his door, and hopped out. He appeared taller than she remembered from this morning, and his shoulders looked broader.

Beth forced her attention back to the help-wanted ads. There were only two notices. The feed store was offering a heavy labor job and a rancher on the west side of town needed someone to clean horse stalls.

Not even a waitress job.

She sighed and continued staring at the now blurring print.

"Evenin'."

Trace's easy greeting traveled gently up her spine, and Beth fought the shiver that threatened.

She lowered the paper. "Hello," was all she could manage.

He nodded back. The dark, slightly curly hair at his nape, still damp from a shower, peeked out from his cowboy hat. He'd put on a clean shirt, a dark blue one that accented his tanned skin.

Trace Barlow was neat from head to toe. Despite his masculine demeanor, he looked like a kid being called to the principal's office.

She couldn't help but smile as she fought the unfamiliar attraction for the man standing in front of her.

"Carol's not here?" he asked, in his deep voice.

"No." Beth glanced at her watch again. "You're early." She folded the paper and looked toward the horizon, wishing her heart would beat normally.

"Any news?"

"What?" She looked back to Trace.

He'd hitched a booted foot on the step and

leaned against the railing. A tiny speck of blood on the right side of his jaw told her he'd shaved too close. His skin looked smooth, and his crisp aftershave filled the air around her.

He nodded toward the newspaper. "Any news worth knowing about?"

She hadn't read anything but the help-wanted ads. Her son had been sullen and moody after Trace's visit, and she'd spent most of her afternoon trying to talk to him.

"Did you and Ben have a good visit?" she asked directly, hoping Trace's answer would shine some light on why her son had been so unhappy.

"He got a little upset when I told him I wasn't going to be his mentor. Thought I didn't like him."

Beth nibbled at her bottom lip. There were times when she didn't understand her son. "Well, he's at that age."

Trace nodded. "He showed me his artwork. The kid's good."

"That means he likes you. He's very private about his talent."

"He also told me the kids in Dallas made fun of him, called him a sissy because he can draw." Trace studied her, his dark eyes velvety in the fading evening light.

"He never said anything to me. I wonder why. I could have done something." Beth's heart began its familiar ache for her son. Kids could be so cruel. Long ago they'd teased her because her dad had taken off.

"Kid probably didn't want to worry you. I wouldn't be troubled by it. Boys tend to be protective of their mamas."

Beth felt a smile slip across her lips as a cool breeze from the west swirled around her. In the last year, Ben had teetered on the edge of being a sullen preteen. There were times it was difficult to remember her son was growing up.

"Did you find a job?" Trace nodded toward the paper still in her hand.

"Not unless I can dig a ditch or work in a barn."

"You don't look quite strong enough for heavy labor." His eyes narrowed, crows'-feet cutting his temples, as his gaze drifted over her.

The darned butterflies she'd been fighting took flight in her chest. Beth inhaled and folded the newspaper.

"I might have to dig ditches if I don't find something soon." Beth spoke to distract herself, but quickly wished she hadn't. She shouldn't be telling this man her problems.

"You've got a nice piece of property here. Took a look around this morning with Ben."

"Yes. My father came out here to raise cattle." Till the end of his life, her father was still searching for another pipe dream to fulfill—something other than his family to make him happy.

"Too bad you didn't get to know your dad before he passed away." Trace's dark gaze grew more serious as the pink and orange sunset surrounded them.

"My dad wasn't a family man." Why in the world was she being so open with Trace about her nonexistent relationship with her father? She studied Trace for a moment. Was it his velvety gaze that made it so easy to talk to him? Or was it the concern she always heard in his voice?

No matter. She certainly wasn't going to tell this cowboy her life story.

"Must be tough for you to come all the way out here not knowing anyone." Trace's dark gaze softened more.

"I didn't want to move, but when Ben got in trouble I didn't feel I had a choice. My son comes first," Beth blurted.

Trace smiled. "Nice to see someone putting their kid first. Don't come across that much nowadays."

The early evening breeze again brought a wave of his aftershave to Beth. Trace smelled so good—clean and comfortable.

He shifted and eyed the newspaper again. "Maybe there'll be something next week. I think Junior's Cafe is still looking for a waitress. Thought I saw a sign in the window. Of course, that's not like managing an office."

"I'll drive into town tomorrow." Beth's stomach dipped. She only had enough money to last, at the most, a month, so at the moment a waitressing job sounded wonderful.

"You need a job pretty bad, don't you?"

She laughed at his directness. Trace Barlow didn't waste any time with chitchat. "I do if I plan to feed Ben. I don't know if you know this, but boys that age like to eat—*a lot.*"

Trace climbed the three porch steps and stood next to her, his thumbs still hooked in his pockets. "Yeah. When I was ten, nothing could fill me up. Only gets worse. At sixteen I could flatten four Dairy Queen burgers when I could get my hands on them."

She turned toward him. "When you could get your hands on them?" She didn't want to be nosy, but she couldn't help herself with Trace standing so close.

They stared at each other for two heartbeats. The brim of his hat accented his brown eyes and the thick lashes lining them. There was something so calm about the man. Beth wondered where it came from. The few men she'd dated in Dallas had seemed uptight, so nervous.

It was obvious Trace Barlow was comfortable in his own skin.

"I've been on my own since I was fifteen. Hamburger money was about all I had, and sometimes not even that," he said without any hesitation or sorrow.

"Fifteen is pretty young to have to feed yourself. How in the world did you do it?"

"I made my eating money with the rodeo. I started working around arenas when I was ten, then competing at twelve. Then when my old man took off, the money came in handy."

Trace's story was the opposite of Ray's. Her in-laws had nurtured their son, supported his rodeo career until he started making big money. "You must be good."

"I've never won big, but the money kept me from going hungry and naked." Trace smiled, then laughed. The hearty sound surrounded Beth.

Beth tried not to imagine his bare skin glowing in the sunset or his tanned, muscled chest. Her gaze drifted to the opening of his cowboy shirt. A tuft of dark, curly chest hair peeked out. For a fleeting moment, she envisioned her fingers tangling in the thick matting.

"Ben told me about his daddy. I really had to go back, but I remember Ray Morris."

His words brought her out of her fantasy. Beth felt light-headed and embarrassed for not paying attention. Of course Trace would know of Ray. Every rodeo rider in the country had heard of Ray, his talent, his NFR championships . . . and his death.

Beth swallowed hard. Trace was a risk taker, too—just like Ray. The last thing she should be doing was daydreaming about running her fingers across his chest.

"Ben told you what I think of cowboys." Her voice sounded too harsh, but Trace stirred something in her she didn't want to feel, and the only thing to do was fight it. She'd been down this road before and made all the wrong choices.

She wasn't going to do it again.

"Yeah." Trace said nothing more, as though he knew she was thinking cowboys were pretty much pond scum.

Beth placed her fingers against her throat.

Good Lord! She was the silliest woman in the world. The man had only shared a memory about hamburgers with her. She'd been the one to imagine him naked as a jaybird. She had to get hold of herself.

"Where's Ben?" Trace asked.

"He went down to the barn late this afternoon and wouldn't come up for supper. Said he wasn't hungry."

"I was pretty moody at that age, too." The corners of Trace's lips lifted. "I like your son. He's a nice kid."

Her heart softened a little. "Ben's great when he not grousing around."

They both chuckled, and the cool breeze lifted their laughter up, braided it together, and carried the melodic sound across the yard.

Yes, she was just being silly. Soon she wouldn't even have to see Trace. "Sometimes I don't know what's wrong with Ben."

Trace hitched his thumb under the brim of his hat and pushed it back a little. His eyes narrowed. "I don't know anything about kids, that's for sure, but Ben talked about his old man a lot down at the barn. He misses him."

Beth's mouth grew dry. She swallowed over the lump in her throat. "I've tried to make up for his not having a dad."

"I don't know if you can, but Ben'll be all right."

"I hope so. If Ray hadn't been so famous in the rodeo circuit, maybe Ben wouldn't miss him so much." Beth crossed her arms, hugged herself, and shifted her gaze out to the horizon. For years she'd worried about her son's desire to follow in his father's footsteps.

Trace's hand touched her shoulder before she could take another breath. His warmth wove over her skin and caused a deep commotion inside of her. The contact felt so good, yet she knew it shouldn't. She turned slightly and met his stare.

"Hey, my daddy took off on me. I still miss him, and he wasn't even a hero. Your kid is always gonna care about his dad." Sincerity underlined Trace's words.

He was right, and she knew it. Ben *should* think about Ray. But when he talked about being in rodeos and taking chances like Ray had . . .

Beth shook her head. She wasn't about to lose her son to the rodeo. She'd come out to Oak Creek because city life was hurting Ben, and she was determined to make the change work. She was sure it would have if Trace Barlow hadn't come into their lives.

Trace mentally kicked himself. Hell, here he was giving this woman advice about raising Ben when he didn't know anything about family or kids.

But when he'd seen the worry in Beth's eyes, he'd only wanted to make her feel better.

She stepped back and faced him, her eyes wide, her chest expanding with each breath. The roundness of her breasts stretched the T-shirt she was wearing. Even in the dimming light, Trace could see the hard peaks of her nipples.

Despite his good sense, he imagined her without the shirt, lying on clean sheets, her angel-like hair splayed against the pillow, her skin soft and sweetly scented.

God, she had a beautiful body. He wanted to take this woman in his arms and kiss her. The renegade urge pushed what was left of his breath back in his throat.

The sound of a car turning onto the gravel ripped through the silence and saved him. Trace stepped back and slipped his fingertips in his pocket.

A tan Suburban flew down the road toward the house.

"That's Carol," he announced before his mouth turned too dry.

"I'll go pour some iced tea. Sweetened?"

"Nope." Trace watched as Beth crossed the small space to the screened front door. Her straight hair swung easily and brushed against her shoulders. He let his eyes travel farther. The long, filmy skirt she wore accented her perky bottom, and the light from the house turned the material sheer, allowing him to admire her long, shapely legs.

A warm, syrupy sensation rose from his loins and squeezed into his belly. Trying to fight the feeling, Trace ground his back teeth. He didn't need to be ogling this woman. But in spite of himself, his gut tightened more, and his attention stayed glued to Beth.

The screen door slammed shut and she was gone. He missed her and felt like a fool, all at the same time. The woman took his good sense away.

"So as you can see, Judge Kelly, it's really a good idea to take Ben out of the mentoring program." Beth held her breath. She'd just spent fifteen minutes explaining why the mentoring situation with Trace wouldn't work and how she was confident, now that Ben was away from Dallas, he'd be fine.

Beth shifted her attention from Carol Kelly's noncommittal face to Trace. She couldn't read his expression, either. He'd only nodded once in a while.

The way he'd talked this morning about being so busy, not knowing anything about how to mentor, she'd expected him to jump right in and help her convince the judge.

"Well, I haven't even met Ben. I should do that, Mrs. Morris."

"Please, call me Beth."

Carol nodded. "Meeting Ben is the reason I

came out to Oak Creek. If I'm going to monitor his case, I need to talk to him."

"Yes, but . . ." Beth turned to Trace again. He was still staring at her, his dark eyes unreadable. Beth swallowed hard. "Ben's down at the barn. He's doing fine now that we're settled."

"He likes horses?" Carol asked.

"No, he paints, draws. I let him make a studio out of the barn office. I encourage him as much as I can." She had to convince Carol they didn't need Trace in their life. Long ago she'd made up her mind to raise Ben alone. Besides, she didn't want this cowboy around stealing her sanity and talking to Ben about rodeos.

"That's wonderful. Young people need hobbies to give them self-esteem." Carol glanced at Trace and smiled. " 'Course, Trace had the rodeo competitions when he was a boy."

Trace's expression didn't change, but Beth could swear she saw a slight flush rise to his cheeks. Her heart hitched a little. She should be thinking of more ways to convince the judge Ben didn't need anyone but his mother in his life.

"Ben is different from the kids you come in contact with, Carol. He's been painting and drawing since he was very young. This is the first time he's been in trouble, and I took him out of that environment. I can raise my son by my—"

"Before you go on, I really need to talk to your son." The judge held up her hand.

Beth glanced at Trace. He was staring at the

last bit of sun sinking behind the horizon. She wanted to shake him. He'd promised to help her.

"I know you have your son's best interests at heart and you're a good parent, but . . ."

Beth's head pounded. She could raise Ben on her own, and she didn't want anyone involved, especially a man who put his life on the line the way Ray had.

"My first responsibility is to Ben and his progress. The probation officer felt he needed a male role model in his life."

"Carol, Beth has a point," Trace said in a controlled tone. "The boy should have a mentor who knows what he's doing. I'm not that guy."

Beth breathed a sigh of relief. Although she liked Carol, she wasn't making any headway with the woman. Now maybe Trace would help.

"The kid needs someone who knows something about art. You know I'm not that person," Trace said.

"You can't encourage him?" Carol's gaze turned steely.

"Well, yeah, but if his mother doesn't want a mentor for her boy, then I understand—and you should, too."

Beth wasn't planning on missing this chance. "Trace is right. He's not the right man."

"I think he is," Carol announced emphatically.

Beth's head pounded more, and she rubbed her temples. She was losing this battle, and she had to do something. "I'm very capable of taking care of Ben."

Carol's gaze softened a little. "I believe that, Beth, but mentoring has been proven to help kids who've lost a parent, especially boys who are having trouble."

Trace cleared his throat and leaned forward. "I don't know anything about mentoring. You know what a crappy family I came from. Besides, how can I help a kid like Ben? I don't know a Picasso from a potato chip."

Beth heard the hurt in Trace's voice, and she automatically looked at him. His brows were knitted with worry.

"M-o-o-o-m," Ben called as he raced across the grass to the house.

All eyes turned toward the steps that Ben took at a gallop. His white T-shirt, splattered with a rainbow of colors, announced itself. He shifted his troubled gaze from Beth to the stranger. Suddenly he saw Trace and smiled.

"Hey, Trace." Ben lifted his hand, high-fived Trace, then laughed.

Beth stood and smoothed her son's hair. "You've been down at the barn a long time. Hungry?"

"Nah, I painted a picture of the house. It's awesome."

"Hey, Mister Artist, the paint's flaking on this house. Try putting a brush on those eves." Trace nodded upward then grinned at Ben and chuckled.

Ben stuck out his chin. "Man shouldn't say

anything he can't back up—like you told me this morning."

"True. You're a fast learner. I like that in a guy," Trace said. Ben grinned at Trace's praise.

Although Beth hated to admit it, Trace seemed very comfortable around Ben, and it was obvious how her son felt. Beth's heart pounded in her chest. For the first time in a week, she saw true happiness on Ben's face.

Carol cleared her throat, stood, and stepped toward Ben. "I'm Carol Kelly, the person in charge of your probation."

Beth wrapped an arm around her son's shoulders as a protective urge snaked through her heart. Surely the judge would rescind her order. She and Ben would make it on their own just fine.

"Hello," Ben said, fear filling his gaze.

"I'm only here to talk to you about the mentoring program."

Ben's chin raised a little. "Yeah?"

"I appointed Trace to be your mentor. What do you think of that?"

"I like him a lot," Ben said. "He's a great guy."

The judge studied Ben for a moment, then switched her attention to Beth and Trace. A smile graced her lips. "Glad to hear it, Ben. Trace is going to stay your mentor."

Beth's heart sank into her stomach. Things were not working out at all.

"Yahooo!" Ben said. "How 'bout that, Trace?

You and me get to spend time together. Maybe you can show me a few roping tricks. Hey, Mom, I'm hungry."

"I left a plate on the stove." Beth could hardly get out the words.

Ben tore away from her embrace and made his way to the screen door, then stopped and turned. "Trace, you want somethin' to eat?"

"Nah, you go on," Trace said quietly, but kept his gaze on Beth.

"OK. See ya tomorrow." Ben opened the screen door and ran into the house.

Everything is going to work out just fine. That was the last statement Carol had made before she climbed into her utility vehicle. Trace wasn't sure she was right.

He watched her taillights all the way down the gravel road before he turned back to Beth. His heart lunged in his chest when he saw the look of disappointment and discouragement in Beth's blue eyes. Her delicate fingers tangled in her hair as she swept it away from her cheek.

The woman was just trying to be a good mother, and he respected her for that. All he wanted to do at the moment was bring her into his arms and tell her to quit worrying.

Beth's hands came to rest against the curves of her hips. She sat on the porch chair and pulled her knees up under her chin. Her skirt billowed out in front of her.

"Why wouldn't she listen to me?" she asked in the softest voice he'd ever heard.

"Ben's honesty was our downfall."

"*Our*? How can you include yourself in this battle? You sure didn't say much." Her hands covered her face and she rubbed her eyes. A sigh fell from her lips, and she wrapped her arms around her legs once again. "Did you have to be so friendly with Ben?"

"I didn't mean to cause any trouble. Shoot, I like your kid."

Beth's gaze softened a little and tore at his heartstrings. "I haven't seen my son so happy in a long time, talking, laughing. Ben likes you, too. The judge could see it."

A bit of her beautiful smile appeared and Trace tried to push the attraction he felt back, but it didn't work.

The satiny lights from the house surrounded her and made Beth's blue eyes turn the color of a Texas morning sky. Her lips appeared a softer color—like the pink roses he'd seen once in a bouquet officials had given the Mesquite Rodeo Queen.

The vision stole any of his rational thoughts.

Suddenly Beth curled her right hand into a fist and she pounded the arm of the wooden chair. "I'm very capable of taking care of Ben. And now with you, Ben's going to want to compete in rodeos. It's too dangerous. He might . . ."

Trace heard the agony in her voice and his

heart slammed against his ribs. He stepped closer and knelt beside her.

"Hey, nobody thinks you aren't a good parent. You've sacrificed a lot for Ben, and I promise I won't talk rodeo. You've got my word on that one."

The gentle evening breeze lifted her scent and carried it to him. He felt dizzy and unsure of himself. Trace knew he should move away from her, but he couldn't.

She swiped at her eyes and lifted her chin. Obviously she was on the verge of bawling. Trace allowed himself to touch her shoulder and massage the tight muscles. "It's gonna be OK."

She looked at him. "This is ridiculous. I'm just mad, that's all."

Trace straightened and stepped back, confused at why he'd knelt beside her in the first place. "Yeah, ridiculous. I've got my own problems." But he was still close enough to feel the heat radiating from her, and his mixed-up feelings were driving him crazy.

"Well, I'm just going to have to make the best of this situation. It's only for fifty hours. That'll go fast." She stood.

"Yeah, make the best of it," was all he could say. He combed his fingers through his hair, then jammed them in his pockets.

But when her tongue darted out and moistened her bottom lip, Trace knew there was going to be no *best* of this situation.

A deep, thick need for Beth rose into his

belly, and he wondered how in the hell he was going to keep his mind on anything but Beth Morris.

FIVE

Beth looked in the mirror and touched the white collar of the pink polyester uniform she'd slipped into a minute ago. She smoothed the short skirt and wished it was a little longer. The shiny material cut three inches above her knees and made her look like a piece of bubble gum.

She studied her reflection, then laughed. Thank goodness she'd found a job. Two mornings ago, after she'd dropped Ben off at school, she'd driven down Branding's Main Street and spied the help-wanted sign in the window of Junior's.

Fifteen minutes later she was an official employee of the only restaurant in town.

Things were looking up!

Junior Lester, the owner of the restaurant, had been encouraging and pretty flexible about her hours. She'd only have to work till four, so Ben would only be alone for an hour in the afternoons.

Beth smiled again.

Things were going well with her son, too. He

had actually been happy the past two days—laughing and telling her silly knock-knock jokes. Beth took a deep breath.

Jokes his *mentor* had told him.

Trace Barlow had driven out to the ranch every day since their meeting with Carol and spent two hours with her son. They either walked around the ranch and fixed fences or hung out in the barn.

Beth nibbled her bottom lip. She was getting used to the confusion gripping her stomach when she thought of Trace Barlow—or, worse, when she saw him.

Yet Trace was making a difference in her son's life, and that was all that mattered to her.

He'd taught Ben how to mend a fence and encouraged him to paint more. Ben had told her, with a large amount of pride, that they'd made a cover for the open well by the barn. The boy seemed to be getting along just fine.

But she and Trace danced around each other like two cats in a closet.

Beth glanced in the mirror and smoothed the stray wisps of hair back from her face. She and Trace said hello when he came to see Ben, but then, by some unspoken rule, they kept their distance.

That was just fine with her. She was certain she'd never get used to the way she felt around Trace.

"M-o-o-o-m!"

The screen door squeaked open, then slammed shut.

Beth chuckled. Ben could really enter a room!

"I'm right here, honey." She walked into the living room.

"Geez, Mom. Where'd you get that getup? You look like something out of *Laverne & Shirley.*"

Beth laughed again and turned toward the kitchen. "It's not a fashion statement, I know, but it's what I have to wear if I'm going to work as a waitress at Junior's while you're in school."

"I think she looks pretty."

The now-familiar deep voice stopped Beth in her tracks. Trace must have come in with Ben a minute ago, and she hadn't noticed. Beth whirled around and her hand automatically found her heart.

Trace stood by the front door, a smile on his face, his hat in his hand, his blue cowboy shirt tucked into his worn jeans.

"Oh, I didn't know you were here." Her heart picked up its pace and beat far too fast.

"I met Ben at school and drove him home. I need to take care of some things later this evening, but I didn't want to miss my mentoring time."

"I didn't mean . . . you're perfectly welcome . . . and thanks for giving him a ride. He doesn't like the school bus." She was actually stuttering. What in the world was wrong with her?

"Mom, I'm hungry," Ben called from the kitchen.

Beth had been so distracted she hadn't noticed Ben had left the room. "I'll be right there, honey." She turned back to Trace and took a deep breath. "Ben is always starving when he comes home from school."

Trace nodded. "Aren't most kids?"

Ben raced back into the living room. "Hey, Mom, why are you still wearing that dorky dress if you don't have to work right now?"

Beth looked down at the blaze of hot pink and then at Trace. He was staring at her. She pushed at the skirt and wished she could make the hem grow three inches. "I was making sure it fit."

Trace raised a brow. "Looks to me like it fits just fine."

"Yeah, it's OK. Why are girls always worried about their stupid clothes?" Ben looked at Trace.

"Ben, give me a few minutes to change—"

"I can take Ben into town for a snack. I need to go into town, anyway," Trace said, his velvety brown eyes softening as they stayed glued to Beth.

Darn! Why did her skirt have to be the size of a postage stamp? And why, oh, why, did her heart have to start beating so hard?

"Oh, I wouldn't expect you to do that. I'm just not very organized this afternoon. I'm starting work tomorrow and I've got so many things to do." Beth let her hand feather around the living room. She'd spent two hours trying to balance her checking account this morning, then another two cleaning.

"Mom, I could sure use something to eat." Ben came and stood between them.

"It's no problem. I won't overfeed him." Trace reached out and ruffled Ben's already messy hair.

Ben laughed. "Yeah, Mom, is it OK? Maybe Trace and I can check out where you'll be working."

For the last few days Ben had been so cheerful, and his teachers had told her he was doing better in school. She didn't want to admit it, but Trace's mentoring seemed to be working.

"It's fine, but you need to be back for dinner. I know you have a lot of homework."

"Yay! Hey, Trace will you show me your ranch? The other day you promised. Maybe we can practice some roping tricks."

With her son's words, a hitch started in her heart. At times she forgot about Trace's being on the rodeo circuit.

"The ranch, yes. The tricks, no." Trace put his hat on and angled it the way he always did.

"You have homework, Ben. You're behind in math and it won't be too long before the year ends." She tried to keep her voice level, but found it almost impossible.

The thought of Ben's learning anything about the rodeo scared her to the bone. She crossed the room to the stack of paperwork on the couch. If anything would get her mind off what she was thinking right now, it was her money problems.

Trace pushed on the screen door and nodded toward Ben. "Why don't you head on out to the truck? I want to talk to your mom for a minute."

"Sure, Trace. See ya, Mom."

The slam of the screen door let Beth know her son had gone outside. She sat on the couch and thumbed through her check register. Thank God she'd gotten the job at Junior's. They were down to their last hundred dollars.

"I won't keep him out long, and when I bring him back I'll help him with his math," Trace said, his voice low.

Beth looked up. Trace was standing next to the couch. She blinked back the tears that were getting ready to splash on her lap.

She was not going to give in to a crying jag if she could help it, even if her financial life was hanging by a hundred-dollar thread and she was still worried about Ben.

"Fine, but you don't have to spend all that time. I'm very capable of helping Ben with his homework. And please don't show him any roping tricks. It will just encourage him about wanting to be part of some rodeo."

"I wasn't planning on it," Trace said flatly. "I don't have the time, and I know you wouldn't want me to. Kid got it into his head I would, that's all."

Beth studied her clasped hands. She shouldn't have said what she did. According to Ben, Trace only talked about raising cattle and Ben's artwork when they were together.

"I know. I guess I'm just nervous about my job and my finances." Beth laughed nervously and pressed her moist palms against her pink polyester skirt.

"Don't be nervous. Junior's a good guy. You'll make OK money at the cafe."

She shrugged. She hadn't wanted to reveal any more problems to Trace, but the words had just slipped out. Every time she was around this man, she said things she didn't want to say.

"Thanks for taking Ben. It'll give me time to clean up the living room and get out of this uniform."

Beth stood and pushed the skirt down her thighs. Tonight she'd lower the hem as much as she could. "Bubblegum pink is going to take some getting used to." She made the mistake of looking at Trace.

Why in the world did Trace have to have deep brown eyes that held such concern? And why, when he looked at her, did she have to feel *so* confused?

"If I get a vote in this, I think the dress makes you look mighty cute." Without another word, he pushed the screen door open and walked down the steps to his truck.

* * *

Trace would have kicked himself if he could have. Why in the heck did he have to comment on how good Beth looked in the waitress uniform? He tightened his grip on the steering wheel and knew the answer.

Because he'd been thinking about her all week. His jaw clenched, and he gripped the steering wheel even harder. He'd been telling himself for days he didn't need to be mooning after Beth Morris.

His body wasn't listening.

Even though the pink uniform wasn't modern, it couldn't hide Beth's great body, and the short skirt accented her long, shapely legs.

"Hey, Trace, what did you do today?" Ben asked.

The boy's question brought his attention back to the cab of his pickup. Trace glanced over at Ben and gave him a grin. "Mended fences, practiced a little, mended more fences, and then practiced roping some more."

Ben laughed and Trace felt his chest expand. He hadn't screwed up the mentoring yet. Although he didn't know what the hell he was doing, their visits seemed to be going all right. The kid seemed pretty happy.

But it was all just luck. He'd proved to himself a long time ago he didn't know a darned thing about family and never would. His marriage had broken up before it had really gotten started, all because of him.

"What did you do today? Chase the pretty girls at school?" He treated Ben like he'd wanted to be dealt with years ago.

Ben shook his head. "Girls! No way."

Trace laughed. "You'll think differently in a few years."

"Nah. I don't get them. They're always combing their hair or giggling. Why can't they be more like guys?"

Trace laughed again. "Hey, bud, one day you're gonna be happy they're just the way they are. Girls are confusing, but so are boys to girls."

Beth, in her cute-as-a-button uniform, danced into his thoughts, and he swallowed hard. Trace fought the image, but he couldn't push it back. She'd looked too pretty when she'd suddenly spotted him in the living room and her eyes flashed that blue color he couldn't describe. And when her chest rose and fell, hell, he almost walked across the living room and kissed her right then and there.

"I'm never gonna like girls. But they do smell good sometimes," Ben said.

Beth's flowery scent and something else he couldn't put his finger on attacked his thoughts. "Yeah," was all he could say.

"Girls would be OK if they didn't cry all the time. Yesterday Jessica Smith cried her eyes out on the playground, just like a baby."

"Girls sometimes cry, Ben. You'll get used to it . . . maybe." Trace added the last words to be honest. He'd never get used to women, especially ones like Beth Morris.

"My mom was bawling last night. She didn't think I could hear her, but I did. See, Trace, women, they're always crying like babies."

Ben's hands were gripped into fists and Trace knew automatically his mother's crying bothered the kid. He gulped in the thick, moist air. Beth's tears weren't what he wanted to think about, either. "Why was she crying?"

"Don't know. She was looking at some papers. Then a little later I heard her crying in her room," Ben said, staring at Trace. "Don't worry about it. She seems pretty happy today."

Great! Now the kid was mentoring him! But he still couldn't shake the bad feelings. It had to be money problems, or maybe she was lonely. It couldn't be easy on a woman to move out to a ranch she knew nothing about.

"Maybe the job at Junior's will help out," Trace said to Ben, hoping to make himself and the kid feel better.

"Will she make a lot of money?"

Trace couldn't help but laugh. "Afraid not. Not many big tippers hang out at Junior's. Just ropers and rednecks."

"Then she's not gonna stop bawling. I think she's got problems." Ben pressed the button on his window and the glass slid down. Thick afternoon air blew into the pickup.

"Someday I'm gonna win the NFR and give my mom all the money she can spend," Ben announced loudly. "Just like my dad. I'm gonna be a rodeo star!"

Trace gritted his teeth. He'd promised Beth he wouldn't encourage Ben about the rodeo. "You need to concentrate on your artwork."

"You sound just like Mom." Ben pushed the window button again. The window slid up and the breeze disappeared.

"Still hungry?" Trace asked as he pulled his pickup into Junior's.

"You bet I am." Ben was out of the truck before Trace could get his seat belt undone. He chuckled. Had he ever had that much energy?

They walked into Junior's. Three ranchers sat at a scarred Formica table. They nodded to Trace.

"Hey, Trace, find another place to lease?" one of the men asked as Trace and Ben headed for the back booth.

"Nah, not sure what I'm gonna do," Trace shouted across the room. "If you hear of anything, let me know." Trace's gut tightened. He'd thought of asking Beth about leasing her land, but that wasn't any way to keep his distance from her. He thought about her all the time as it was. What would it be like if he lived on the same property?

Yet if he didn't find some land soon, he was going to have to sell his cattle.

"You gotta leave the house you're renting, too?" one of the other men asked.

"Yep. Entire place is being bought by a speculator."

He and Ben slid across from each other on the plastic booth seats and ordered apple pie. "Put extra whipped cream on this guy's. He needs to feed his muscles," Trace told the waitress.

Ben looked at Trace as the waitress walked away. "You're going to move from Branding?" His blond brows knitted together.

Trace studied the kid. Now where had that come from? Trace scratched his head. "Why would I move away from Branding?"

Ben pointed toward the men across the room. "You can't find a place. I don't want you to move."

Trace laughed. It was funny what kids picked up. "I'm not moving. I've just got to find some land in the area for my cattle to graze on. The place I rent was sold, but that doesn't mean I'm leaving town."

As Ben digested Trace's words, his smile returned.

"Besides, Ben, I can't leave you till I'm through mentoring. And I want to see how some of your artwork turns out. Have you finished that picture of your mama yet?"

"Almost. Can't wait to give it to her. You've got to come to her birthday party. Will you?"

"I'm plenty busy, Ben."

Even though his words wiped the smile off Ben's face, Trace knew he didn't need to put himself closer to Beth Morris. No, he didn't want to torture himself and watch her eyes sparkle when she opened Ben's gift, or listen to her sweet voice or fight her pretty scent as it climbed all over him.

Trace drew in a deep breath. Yep, it was best he kept his distance from Beth.

Beth watched as Trace pointed to the math book. He and Ben were sitting at the kitchen table, and her son was laughing.

She couldn't believe her ears.

Seeing Ben enjoy math homework seemed like an episode from *The X Files*. When he and Trace had returned from town, Ben had begged his mentor to stay and eat dinner with them. Trace had finally accepted.

Thank goodness she'd managed to change out of the uniform before they'd come back from town.

"If you had a thousand head of cattle and you divided it by thirteen what would you get?" Trace asked, then sat back in the oak kitchen chair.

"A herd of cattle," Ben answered and giggled for a full minute, then used his pencil and paper to divide. "Seventy-six and twelve left over."

"That's right. Now let's take girls. If you had

thirteen girls and you kissed each one thirteen times how many kisses would you give out?"

Trace looked at Beth, and her heart flip-flopped like a teenager's. She tried to tell herself she was only feeling this way because she was happy for Ben, yet she didn't believe it, even though Ben was smiling and having fun.

Trace was making her feel off balance.

"Kisses! Are you kidding? I'm not kissing anybody!" Ben leaned back in his chair and crossed his arms, mirroring Trace's body language.

Beth swallowed over the lump in her throat. Was this how their life would have been if Ray had lived? She didn't know the answer. They'd been too young to marry. She wasn't even sure they would have survived ten years together.

She shook her head. She didn't need to be thinking about the past right now.

"Kisses or no kisses, we'll have to continue tomorrow, Ben." Trace checked his watch.

Beth glanced back to the kitchen clock. Where had the time gone? "Ben, it's bedtime."

"Aw, I don't want to go to bed. I want to do more math with Trace."

"Mom's right, partner. Better hit the rack. You've got school tomorrow."

With just a little more complaining, Ben washed up and headed for bed. Before he turned out his light, he yelled good-bye to Trace, who was heading for the front door.

" 'Night, Ben. I'll see you tomorrow." Trace put on his cowboy hat and nodded to Beth.

"Thanks for supper. It was nice having a home-cooked meal."

Beth nibbled on her bottom lip. She'd enjoyed the adult company at the dinner table, and Ben had actually had fun with his math homework. She really owed the man a thank you.

"I'm glad you stayed for dinner, even though Ben twisted your arm. In the last week he's been so happy. He really likes you."

Trace dipped his chin a little. "I like the kid, too. Don't know if I'm doing this mentoring thing right, but it seems to be working out OK." He pushed on the screen door. "I enjoyed supper."

Beth followed him out the door. She still hadn't thanked him for helping Ben with his math or encouraging him about his artwork. Since Trace had started mentoring, anytime Ben had a free moment, he'd gallop down to the barn to paint. Beth knew it had something to do with Trace and the time he spent with her son.

"Trace," she called out before he could start down the steps.

He turned, his eyes narrowing.

Her heart pounded. The light from the house outlined him. For some reason, he looked larger than life as he stood framed against the inky Texas sky, stars sparkling all around him.

"Did I forget something?" He started back across the porch.

"No. No. I just wanted to thank you for helping Ben with his math homework. He's like a different person when you're around. Usually when I help him, he complains and whines so much we end up fighting and I send him to bed."

Beth combed her fingers through her hair. There were so many parenting skills she lacked, and at times she wished she had someone to give her encouragement.

Trace laughed and leaned against the porch banister. "I would think most kids are like that. Heck, I'm a stranger to Ben. That's the reason he doesn't fight with me."

"It seems so easy for you."

"Don't kid yourself. You're doing a fine job raising him."

At Trace's words, a warmth filled her body. She'd spent many sleepless nights wondering if she was doing right by Ben. "You don't know how good it feels to hear that. Single parenting can be tough. I'm always the heavy. Just once I'd like to be able to say, 'Go ask your dad.' "

Trace nodded, then took off his hat and ran his fingers through his hair, his gaze worried. "I'm probably not the best one to ask. I don't know anything about kids. I've just been lucky with Ben."

"I think it's more than luck, Trace. I was having a heck of a time with him before you came into the picture." Beth drew in a deep breath, and the moist summer air surrounded her. To her surprise, her body trembled a little.

She'd only meant to thank him for all he'd done, not start a conversation with the man.

"He's a great kid. You're a good mama." Trace crossed his arms and squared his jaw. "You know how I know that?"

Beth shook her head.

"He worries about you. That shows he loves you."

She stepped toward Trace and laughed a little, her hand finding the middle of her chest. "Ben's concerned about me? Really?" It seemed so odd to hear her child was worried about her.

"Yeah. When we were driving into town this afternoon he told me you'd been crying last night." Trace shifted a little and squared his shoulders. His eyes looked so dark in the half-light of the porch.

Her heart pumped harder. She saw concern etched on Trace's face. Good Lord, what was the matter with her? She shouldn't want the man to worry about her.

But deep down she knew why her heart was pounding so hard. It had been so long since anyone had shown the slightest bit of interest in her and Ben's lives, and tonight it felt good, like a warm bath after a hard day at work.

"Why were you crying?" Trace's voice was just above a rough whisper. His eyes narrowed with more concern and his crow's-feet fanned back to his hairline. His hand found her shoulder and his body heat danced through her tense muscles.

Beth drew in a breath. "I . . . I'm worried about money, that's all."

In the dim porch light, he nodded once and stepped close to her.

Suddenly she was in Trace's strong arms.

SIX

Trace wrapped his arms around Beth so easily, it felt like he'd held her a hundred times before. Ever since he'd met her, he'd imagined holding Beth like this. But reality was better than any of his dreams.

She was warm—soft and curved in all the right places. And when her sweet, feminine scent surrounded him, he felt he could win a thousand rodeo prizes.

He touched her hair. It was as silky as he'd thought it would be. Trace leaned back and looked into Beth's beautiful blue eyes.

A moment later his lips touched hers. To his amazement, her tongue flicked out and wet his bottom lip. He'd only brought her into his arms to comfort her, yet Trace couldn't fight the need the kiss was creating. He pulled her closer, kissing her more, their bodies fitting together perfectly, their lips expressing the need bubbling within them.

Deep down Trace knew he shouldn't be kissing Beth, but at the moment he didn't care what was right or wrong. All he wanted was Beth against him.

She arched and her hips fit against his.

Trace felt like the top of his head might fly off. His tongue searched and plunged into her wet mouth. Their tongues danced against each other. When a sexy moan escaped her sweet lips, Trace knew he was on the ride of his life, and he didn't want to turn back.

Beth heard a noise from the house but pushed it out of her mind. Trace's arms felt utterly magnificent. It had been so long since she'd kissed a man, so long since she'd wanted to be held by a man.

A sharp urgency to kiss him harder and longer overtook her. Trace tasted like everything good, and his warm embrace made Beth feel anything was possible. She moved easily against him, pulling him to her, her mouth opening, inviting him in.

Trace responded by bringing her closer and raining a trail of kisses down her face to the arch of her throat. His tongue flicked out and Beth heard herself moan again.

God, how good it felt to kiss this man.

Another thump from the house transported Beth back to what was real.

Ben's in the kitchen.

The knowledge made her stiffen in Trace's arms. He kissed her again, trailed his lips across her cheeks, and the now-familiar pulsing deep inside her drew Beth back into his arms.

Then her son slammed the refrigerator door.

Beth tore her lips away from Trace's. What had she been thinking?

Yet Trace's arms still encircled her.

With all the willpower she possessed, Beth pressed her palms against his chest.

Trace released her.

They stood in the semidarkness and stared at each other, both breathing hard. Ben's bedroom door slammed and Beth blinked and placed her fingers against her open mouth.

Her lips were warm and slightly bruised from Trace's kisses. His dark eyes were still filled with need for her, and his mouth looked as enticing as it had a few moments before.

She'd just *kissed* Trace Barlow!

And really liked it.

Trace stepped toward her and tried to pull her back into his warm embrace. "Ben's gone back to bed," was all he said.

For a moment she went willingly, but then her body stiffened. "We can't do this."

"*Beth,*" Trace whispered, his voice still raspy. He reached out and touched her arm. Then his strong fingers wrapped around her tense muscles.

Beth suppressed a sigh. God, she enjoyed his touch.

Her mind whirled with the confusing thoughts. Trace was a cowboy who lived and breathed the rodeo. But it had been so long since a man had said her name that way, actually breathed the word and couldn't hide the fact he wanted her back in his arms.

The knowledge made her insides turn white hot and she closed her eyes, bit her bottom lip, and sighed again.

She shook her head and sucked in the moist night air. "Trace, I . . . I need to go inside."

His hand fell away, and she missed his fingers on her arm, missed the closeness his touch created.

Good Lord, what was the matter with her? She'd been down this road before, letting her feelings rule her head. When she'd met Ray, she hadn't thought of the future. Look what that had done. No, she'd never let her emotions rule again.

Trace took a step back, crossed his arms, and stared at her. Even in the dim light, Beth could see his confusion and frustration.

"I don't want you to go in," he said in a low voice.

"This was a mistake. I never should have kissed you."

He studied her for a moment, then spoke. "Yeah, maybe you're right."

Despite the emotions rioting inside her, Beth relaxed a little. Thank goodness he agreed. "Yes, I know I am."

"It was a really *big* mistake." Trace rubbed his thumb over his bottom lip, as if remembering a moment ago when their lips had been sealed together.

Her pulse pounded in her throat as his gaze brought back the intensity of their union. She gulped in more air and demanded her heart quit beating so hard. "I'd rather not talk about it."

He straightened a little and stepped toward her. "I agree. I'd like to experience it again, though."

"Trace!" Beth wasn't sure she could keep herself out of his arms if they talked about this. "I don't know what happened a few minutes ago, but it shouldn't have. And I'm going to make sure it doesn't happen again."

There! Ben had to be her first priority. She couldn't let herself get involved with anyone—especially his mentor.

"Right! I agree. No more kissing," Trace said.

His short, positive response stopped Beth in her mental tracks. She jerked her gaze to his and stared at him. "You agree?"

"Sure. I've got a lot on my mind right now, and I know you do, too. Besides, I'm not sure Carol would classify kissing you as part of my community service." He leaned back against the porch railing and crossed his arms again.

Thank goodness he agreed with her. It would certainly make it easier to stay away from Trace Barlow. "I have enough money problems to make anyone go crazy, not to mention what the judge and Ben might say. I'm not sure why I kissed you, but it won't happen again."

Trace's eyes narrowed again and the crow's-feet deepened across his temples.

"You sound pretty sure of yourself. Why are you so positive?"

Again her body reacted to his deep voice and his confident words. A pulsing started low in her belly and she swallowed hard in an effort to steady herself.

"I just know, that's all. I will not kiss you again. Emotion took over my rational thinking a minute ago."

One minute she'd been standing on the front porch saying thank you, and then she'd been kissing Trace—a rodeo cowboy. Her chest began to ache, and Beth wondered if she'd ever be sure of anything again. When the corners of Trace's lips curved up in a smile, she had to ask him. "Why do you think we kissed?"

Darn it! She shouldn't want to know what Trace Barlow thought about their kissing.

"Hey, don't worry about it. It happened, that's all. There are lots of things I can't explain—like why I feel happy on spring days, and the surprise I always feel when I see a calf born. You can't let yourself worry about stuff you don't understand."

Beth certainly didn't understand her reaction to Trace. "But I don't like not knowing why I do things," she said, hoping Trace could explain her feelings to her.

Trace laughed softly. "People kiss all the time. Most of the time it doesn't have a meaning."

Then his lips slid into a grim line. "Let's just leave it like that."

"But not like *we* kissed! That was pretty out-of-control kissing."

He rubbed the tip of his chin with his fingers and studied her. "True. In fact, you nearly blew my socks off. And me just a cowboy."

Darn, darn, darn! Why hadn't she just dropped this conversation? The way she felt in Trace's arms a few moments ago—well, she knew she couldn't come within three feet of the man and not want to kiss him again.

"Listen, Trace, I realize you think this is funny after my son told you I can't stand cowboys or people in the rodeo." Beth combed her fingers through her hair. Her heart was racing. "But it isn't . . . funny to me." Her voice broke, and she pulled in a breath to steady herself.

She needed to concentrate on Ben and her money problems. Kissing Trace would only complicate her life.

Trace cleared his throat and straightened. "I didn't mean to joke about it, Beth." His tone was serious, and all the humor had vanished from his gaze.

Beth let out the breath she'd been holding and sighed. "Good. Then there shouldn't be a problem. You won't kiss me. I won't kiss you. How many hours do you have left with Ben?" For the life of her, she couldn't remember how many hours Trace had put in.

"A lot. But I think I can stay away till then."

He jammed his fingertips in the slits of his pockets. "I'll see Ben tomorrow. We found some house paint in the barn and we're planning on painting the eves, if that's OK with you."

"Yes, that's fine."

Trace made his way to his truck. She entered the house, then leaned against the doorjamb and sighed.

Kissing Trace a few moments ago had been craziness. She'd let her emotions get away from her, but it wouldn't happen again—that was sure.

Trace gunned the engine of his pickup and slid his tongue over his mouth.

He could still taste Beth on his lips.

The blood pulsed through his body and his manhood pressed hard against his jeans.

Double damn!

He'd never wanted a woman more than he'd wanted Beth a few minutes ago. Now it took all his willpower not to turn off his pickup, jump out, and knock on her door.

Trace ripped off his hat and threw it on the passenger seat. Then he ran his fingers through his hair and gritted his teeth.

The kiss had upset Beth, and that was the last thing he wanted to do to her.

He pressed the button and the driver's window slid down. Fresh air rushed in, but it couldn't begin to cool his hot skin. An image of Beth's pretty blue eyes filled with worry rose in his mind. Trace sucked in more air.

He'd acted so sure and cocky a little while ago when Beth said she was worried about their kiss. But heck, he didn't know what he was doing when he was around the woman.

That bull about people kissing like they had was just that—bull. In his twenty-nine years, he'd never felt such pure need as he had a moment ago.

He pounded the steering wheel with his fist as Beth's worried gaze danced into his mind again.

Tarnation!

He had no business kissing Beth, even though he was so attracted to her his hair hurt every time he looked into her beautiful blue eyes.

She was *nice*. And it was pretty apparent her only interest was to make a home for her son. She had *family* written all over her. He knew one thing to be true: He wasn't and never would be a family man.

Far from it. Hell, he didn't even know what a family was. His mother and old man hadn't managed to keep it together, and after his own marriage had fallen apart after six months, he knew he'd never make a relationship work.

Trace gripped the steering wheel hard. Beth wasn't the type of woman to be drawn into a one-night stand, and he didn't want to cause more worry for her.

He'd concentrate on practicing for the Abilene Rodeo, finding a place to put his cattle, and getting his own ranch back. Maybe in another ten years he'd quit thinking about kissing Beth.

"Hey M-o-o-o-m, look at this!" Ben called over his shoulder as he ran toward the barn.

Beth smiled and picked up her step. For the last few days, Ben had been full of energy and happiness, and Beth knew why.

Trace Barlow.

Beth stopped for a moment and fought the butterflies in her chest. She took a deep breath and told herself she was being silly. The other night out on the porch with Trace had been a mistake, something that would never happen again.

Yet her heart raced with the memory of Trace's lips on hers, his strong arms encasing her body.

"Mom, come on. I want to show you what Trace helped me with."

Her son's demands brought her back from her daydreams, thank goodness. Beth tried to shake off her feelings, but she wasn't successful.

She couldn't stop wondering what would have happened if she hadn't heard Ben in the kitchen the other night.

Beth shivered as an image of what one kiss might have turned into. "Oh, my," she whispered.

"Mom! Come on," Ben called again as he

stopped and turned toward her. "What's the matter, are you sick or something?"

Beth forced herself to quit thinking about Trace. She started to run toward Ben, then realized that wasn't such a good idea. She looked down at her pink-and-white uniform. Ben had been so excited about showing her his work in the barn she hadn't had time to change.

"It's about time. Why were you standing out in the field looking like you didn't know where you were?" Ben asked when she reached him in front of the barn.

Beth felt her cheeks color. There was no way in the world she could tell Ben she'd been thinking about Trace and what had happened.

"Something the matter with you?"

Beth studied her son. His gaze had grown inquisitive. She laughed, feeling like a teenager being questioned by a concerned parent.

"Nothing's wrong. I'm just tired. Waitressing is tough work, harder than I ever thought it would be." Beth told the little white lie because she didn't want her son to fret about her. Things with Ben were going too well.

At first she'd been alarmed about leaving Ben alone for the hour between the time he got out of school and when she could leave Junior's Cafe. But for the last few days, Ben had been coming directly home from school and working on his homework until she could get home.

When she'd come home this afternoon, her son had been waiting at the house, with the TV blaring and an empty milk glass on the coffee table. He hadn't started his homework, but she was pleased he'd followed her instructions not to go down to the barn.

"You look funny, Mom. Same way Suzy Waldron looked before she hurled all over Jason's desk." Ben danced around her. "You should have seen it. The teacher spased out."

"I'm fine, honey." She followed him into the barn. Ten-year-old boys had a way of putting everything in perspective. Yet the excitement she felt when she thought of Trace slid up her spine again and raced through her entire body.

How could one kiss cause so much disruption?

"Don't you think my dad would have liked this place?" Ben asked as he stood in the middle of the barn.

Immediately she stopped thinking about Trace's lips on hers. Ray Morris would not have liked Oak Creek. When she and Ray were together, he'd wanted no responsibilities. But they'd been so young and had given up some of their dreams because she'd let her passion run wild.

"He would have been happy here, right?"

She looked at Ben. Ray had become a mythical figure to her son. Ben didn't understand his father had been young when they'd found out she was pregnant. Ray hadn't been ready for a wife or a child.

From the beginning, Ray had told her he hated the ties that went along with a family. He never understood she'd given up her hopes and dreams, too.

"I'm not sure, honey." And she wasn't, either. Who knew how their life together would have turned out?

"But Dad could have had his horse here and practiced right out there." Ben pointed toward the pasture. "He could have taught me everything he knows. Then all the kids at school would be real jealous." Ben was nodding his head, his blond hair flopping against his forehead as it always did.

Beth's heart ached. Ben needed his father, and he didn't have one because of the chances Ray had taken. Ben had lost so much because of the danger his father had insisted on facing.

Suddenly Ben was dancing around her, grinning to beat the band.

"Come on, Mom. I almost forgot what I brought you down here for. I've got to show you what Trace helped me with." He grabbed her hand and she squeezed his fingers, enjoying her son's excitement.

"What is it?" It was so good to see Ben happy and excited.

"Come on." Ben ran down the short hallway to his art room.

Beth felt herself grin. It had been a long time since her son had been this happy about his paintings.

Ben flung open the door and gave her another grin. "Look!"

She peeked in the room. "What, Ben? More new paintings?" Beth's mouth went dry and she swallowed over the lump in her throat.

"Yeah." He sprinted across the floor. "Trace bought me all this poster board and more paints. Said I shouldn't waste my talent on thinking about competing in rodeos."

Her heart pounded faster. The man didn't have the finances or time to be helping her son with his artwork, yet he did.

"Look, Mom." Ben crossed the space to his easel. "I drew this yesterday."

Ben had drawn a horse standing in front of their house. "A horse! That's your first one, Ben. It's really beautiful." Her son never drew anything western. He'd always said if he couldn't be in rodeos like his father, he didn't want anything to do with horses or cowboys.

"Yeah, thanks. Trace told me about some artist who makes western statues. Thought I'd try a horse, since you won't let me have one." He stared at his work for a moment and then looked at his mother. "It's pretty good, isn't it? 'Course, I won't give up drawing cars and stuff."

"Trace told you about a western artist?" The man never failed to surprise her.

"Yeah. Trace couldn't remember the artist's name when he was talking about him, but then yesterday he brought me a book. Man! He's awesome!"

Ben raced across the room again and found

the gigantic coffee-table book. "See, the guy's good. His name's Remington."

The feelings about Trace she'd been experiencing found her again and careened through her body. Why did the man have to be so . . . nice? His getting Ben the book was just one example of why she was having trouble forgetting him.

"Trace says I can be the next Remington!"

"That's wonderful, Ben," she said, trying to ignore the way she was feeling.

"Yeah!"

Beth had expected Trace to keep his word and not encourage Ben about the rodeo, but she hadn't envisioned him actually inspiring Ben about his artwork.

"I told Trace I'm gonna be in the rodeo just like him, and he says my talent is a gift, or something like that. Says anybody can bounce around on a horse, but not everybody can draw and paint like I do. He doesn't understand I have to be just like my dad."

Just like Ray Morris. Beth drew in a quick breath. She couldn't stand the thought of Ben putting his life in danger and maybe losing him.

"Your father . . ." She wanted to tell Ben his father had taken too many chances, but she stopped herself. How could she hurt her son?

Ben was flipping through the pages of the book, already distracted. "Trace says I should concentrate on drawing. He's said it so many times I told him he was boring."

Ben looked so happy and complete, and it was all because of Trace and what he'd done.

Suddenly she was remembering Trace's mouth on hers, the way it trailed down from her cheek to her throat, his warm breath against her skin. The other night the man had kissed her like there was no tomorrow, touching her body and soul.

With thoughts of their encounter renewed, she actually shivered.

Ben glanced up. "What's the matter with you? You look like you're about to hurl."

Heat flushed her skin, and Beth looked down at the barn floor. Good Lord, just because the man had helped her son was no reason to start fantasizing about the way he had held her and whispered her name against her throat.

Beth took a deep breath and laughed. Her son was right. She was being absolutely silly. Trace was a rodeo cowboy, the last man she'd allow in her life. She'd never expose herself or Ben to the kind of hurt the rodeo could cause.

Getting involved was probably the last thing Trace Barlow wanted. He lived and breathed the rodeo. How in the world could she ask any man to give up what he loved, what made him feel whole?

She'd done that to Ray, and it had caused them both pain.

Beth squared her shoulders. Besides, Trace had told her the kiss was no big deal. Soon his mentoring obligation would be over, and they wouldn't have a reason to see each other. For now, she'd just keep reminding herself that Trace Barlow was not the man for her.

SEVEN

Trace's truck was parked in front of Oak Creek. Although his mentoring had worked out well, Beth knew she'd be glad when she didn't have to worry about seeing Trace anymore.

But without thinking, she glanced in her rear-view mirror and pushed back tendrils of hair that had come loose as she drove down the last bit of highway. Waitressing all day at Junior's was good for her bank account, but not so hot for her hair. Between the steamy heat from the kitchen and the drive home with the window down, she looked frazzled.

Beth reached into her purse for her lipstick, then caught herself. She didn't need to put on lipstick for Trace Barlow.

By staying out of his way and out from under his dark-eyed gaze, she'd managed to keep her distance from Trace.

Beth pulled into her usual parking spot and reasoned she could sneak into the house without seeing Trace. He and Ben were probably down at the barn. He'd leave in an hour or so, and then she'd spend some time with Ben.

When she entered the living room, the first thing she saw was Ben lying on the couch with a dish towel on his forehead.

Her heart raced with fear. "My God, Ben, what happened?" She ran to the couch and knelt down beside her son. His skinned right elbow sported a red blotch of Merthiolate.

"You're gonna catch it when your mama—" Trace's words broke off as he came out of the kitchen. His dark eyes nailed her immediately, and worry lines etched his forehead. "He's OK, Beth. I checked him out when I got here."

"What in the world happened? You weren't showing him anything about the rodeo, were you?" Adrenaline rushed through her body, and Beth felt almost detached from her body.

What if something had happened to Ben while she was gone? She'd never forgive herself.

"I just fell off the stupid fence. Nothing big. I'm fine," Ben said.

"I'm going to take him to the doctor's!" Beth stood.

"Mom, I'm fine. It's nothing."

Trace closed the space between them. "I'll drive Ben and you into town if you want, but I called Doc Henslin and he told me how to check him out. He doesn't have any broken bones. He's just a little skinned up."

Beth closed her eyes and pulled in a much needed breath. Maybe Ben would be all right.

Trace massaged her shoulder with his strong fingers, and she relaxed a little bit.

"He's OK, Beth."

She looked at her son again. "Are you sure?" Ben's eyes were closed and he was so quiet.

"Beth," Trace said quietly, his arm still around her, "don't you know if I thought he was hurt, I would have taken him to the doctor?"

"But why the towel?"

Trace took her elbow and led her to the kitchen. Even with the worry about Ben washing over her, she was aware of Trace's closeness, his clean scent, his body heat. When they reached the kitchen, Trace stopped and turned toward her.

"He said he had a headache, so I found some aspirin, gave him two, and then put ice on his forehead. Thought it would make him feel better. I think he's more worried about your getting mad."

Again she breathed a sigh of relief. "So it's just the scratch on his arm?"

Trace nodded. "And a sore ego. That's all. He's really concerned about getting in trouble with you." Trace rubbed his chin with his forefinger and thumb, then smiled. "Said you treat him like a baby, and he isn't any baby." He chuckled. "I know you worry about him, but the kid's OK."

"I'm going to give him a spanking when he's better."

"Now's there's something he has to look forward to." Trace arched his dark brow and Beth's stomach dipped. The man could make her feel attracted to him at the oddest moments.

"Beth, he's too old to spank." Trace laughed again and shook his head. "But I don't blame you for being angry."

"I told him to stay in the house until I got home. He could have gotten really hurt. And what if you hadn't shown up? Good Lord!"

"All he was doing was climbing the fence out in the east pasture—something about wanting to practice staying on top of a horse—and the thing gave way." He rubbed his chin again. "I already gave him a lecture."

"That damned fence!"

"Yeah, I'll go down and fix it. The wood was probably rotted."

"I'd hire someone to do it, but my money's a little short." She'd had good intentions about a lot of things around the ranch, but all the chores took money and ranching expertise, and she had neither.

"Yeah, I'm singing that song, too."

She looked up at Trace, and he smiled. The man was truly concerned about Ben, and that melted her heart a little. He had his own problems and shouldn't have to worry about hers or Ben's. "Still haven't found a place yet?"

"Nope. There's nothing in the area, and with rodeo practice taking up most of my time . . . Well, I'm a busy man nowadays."

Beth didn't want to think about rodeos. She

needed to worry about her son. "Well, this accident with Ben settles it. I'm going to quit my job." She crossed her arms and hugged herself.

"Can you afford to do that?"

"No!" They were barely making it now from week to week, but she wasn't sure she wanted to share that with Trace. She had to keep the man at arm's length.

"I'll talk to Ben about how important it is to mind you, follow your orders."

"That might help. I'm just so mad at him right now. I must have told him a hundred times to stay in the house."

"Hey." Trace rested his hand on her shoulder.

Beth almost sighed as his warmth and tender touch washed through her body. She looked at him. His dark gaze met hers, and ten thousand butterflies took flight.

Beth closed her eyes to gain control. She didn't need to feel this way about Trace. Yet whenever they were together, the man seemed to know just the right things to say and do.

"Hey, somebody, I need more ice," Ben called from the living room.

"OK, Ben." Trace looked at Beth and smiled. "Once a nurse, always a nurse."

"You don't have to stay. I can take care of him now."

"I haven't finished my hours yet." He nodded back toward the living room. "Besides, I'd better stick around to protect him from you."

She lifted a brow and felt herself smile. "Very

funny. I'm not as mad as I was, but he's got to follow my rules when I'm at work."

"Trace, will you bring me a soda, too?" Ben bellowed from the living room.

With ice and a drink, they walked to the couch together and stared down at Ben. He looked so innocent and young with the towel on his forehead. Beth's heart pounded up into her throat. Good Lord, he was only a child.

"Mom, I'm fine. Don't get all upset. Trace says he used to fall a lot, too. It's what makes a boy a man."

Beth knelt down beside her son. "I'm not angry, just worried. You promised you would stay in the house until I got home." She stroked his hand. Thank goodness he hadn't hit his head.

"It's so boring in the house. I wasn't gonna do anything dangerous, just practice like I was riding a horse. That dumb old fence just broke. I didn't mean to break—"

"Hey, Ben, buddy," Trace knelt next to Beth. "You're lucky you've got a mama to worry about you. And you should follow her rules."

To Beth's surprise, Ben nodded. "Yeah, I know. I remembered what you said." He bit his bottom lip and stared at them. "It's just boring around here. If I had someone around when Mom wasn't . . ." Suddenly he sat up. "Hey, Trace, why don't you move your cattle out here? Then you'd be here a lot more if I got in trouble."

Beth stiffened. Trace did, too. She didn't want

to think about having Trace live at Oak Creek. "Honey, that's not such a good—"

"Why not?" Ben sat up. "Trace doesn't have any place to go, and we've got land. Trace told me our grass is good for cows. What kind of grass is it, Trace? I forgot."

Beth hurriedly stood and almost knocked Trace over. He caught himself and stepped back. "Prime Coastal."

"Yeah, that's it. You could bring your cows here and pay Mom. You could even live in that room over the barn. It's got a bathroom and everything."

"Ben, it won't work," Beth blurted out, still staring at her son, not daring to look at Trace. He had to know Ben's notion wasn't a good idea.

Trace cleared his throat. "I'm close to finding another place. If you just follow your mama's orders, she won't have to quit her job."

With a whoosh, Beth let out the breath she'd been holding.

She certainly did not need Trace Barlow living at Oak Creek.

Trace sat in the porch chair and looked up at the night sky. The velvety darkness was littered with pinpoints of light, and without any interference from a big city, the stars sparkled like diamonds.

The screen door squeaked open, and Trace let himself experience Beth's scent before he looked up. Beth Morris's fragrance always reminded him of good things—nights just like this one, winning a rodeo, or a spring day when he felt he could ride out to the ends of the earth without stopping.

"Thank you for staying for dinner. Ben was really happy you ate with us," she said easily as she moved across the porch to the far side.

Trace absorbed her words before he shifted his gaze. Beth had the kind of voice most women prayed for—deep and husky, yet with a feminine quality that was undeniable.

He lifted his gaze to Beth's. She was five feet away, leaning against the porch banister. After they'd talked to her son this afternoon, she'd excused herself and gone to shower and change her clothes. By the time she'd come back, Ben had it planned that Trace would stay for dinner.

Beth was wearing her usual T-shirt and shorts. Her silky-soft hair was pulled back in an attractive ponytail; her face was scrubbed and beautiful. Trace let his gaze drift over her. With the stars twinkling behind her and the faint light accenting her hair, Beth looked like a dream.

But his attraction to her was more than that. In the last week he'd gotten to know what kind of person she was—caring and good, a woman any man would want to spend time with.

He cleared his throat and forced himself to speak. "I should be thanking you. A home-cooked meal is always a plus for me." His heart was crashing against his ribs and he tried to shift his attention from her but couldn't.

"Well, it wasn't a fancy meal. I'm still working on my cooking skills. I'd try new things, but Ben is kind of picky, so I stick with the basics." She wrinkled her nose a little, then stared at the porch floor.

Trace missed her attention.

"He's a meat and potatoes man, like me. The pork chops and mashed potatoes were fit for a king."

She looked up and smiled. "Thanks."

Every time he was with Beth he couldn't believe some guy hadn't come along and married her. She was so easy to be with.

"What about Ben's dad? Didn't he like fancy cooking?" The question was out before he could stop it. He had no business asking her personal stuff. Soon he'd be gone from her life.

She stared at him for a long moment, then brought her fingers to her throat. "I . . . Ray wasn't home much. He was either practicing, at a rodeo, or out with his friends."

"A lot of practice—that's what it takes to win."

Beth laughed cynically and tipped her chin up to look at the night sky. Suddenly she brought her attention to his again. Her gaze looked different. "Ray Morris lived and breathed the rodeo, and it took his life. Now Ben has to pay the consequences." She crossed her arms.

Trace's gut tightened. He could see the hurt in Beth's eyes, read it in her body language. "It must have been tough for you, being so young and losing him, having to take care of Ben all by yourself."

Her shoulders stiffened. "That was a long time ago." She turned and looked at the stars again. "You don't have very many hours left with Ben. I hope I've thanked you for what you've done."

"He's a good boy."

A smile graced her lips and she looked more than pretty. "Thank you. I like him, too. I hope he realizes it in between the nagging."

"Aw, I'm sure half the time he doesn't even listen."

She laughed. "I know he's good at blocking me out. I'm just his mom." Beth laughed again, and the sound was music to Trace's ears. Everything the woman did was magical. For weeks he'd watched her. She was the kind of woman who would blossom if she had the right man, a man who knew how to be part of her family and loved her with all his heart. A man the opposite of what he was.

His chest tightened. Even though Trace knew he wasn't right for her, it was difficult for him to think of Beth with anyone else.

"You never got serious with anyone in Dallas? Never wanted to marry again?" he asked.

She straightened and shook her head. Starlight danced along her ponytail. "No. Raising Ben and working took up most of my time. I've dated a little, but Ben's about all I can handle. I want to make a home for him, create a family environment. That takes commitment."

"Family . . ." Trace didn't finish. Until he'd met Beth, he wasn't sure he'd known what family really meant.

"And you?" she asked.

"I was married once. It didn't work. I was always practicing, and she didn't like that. In a way I don't blame her. I learned early on I'm not cut out to make a woman happy who needs more than I can give."

"That must have hurt."

"Both of us got hurt." He wasn't about to travel that road again.

"Were you young?" Beth shifted a little, but managed to kept her gaze attached to his.

"Nineteen. Wet behind the ears. Heck, I never had a home, so how could I expect to keep a relationship together?" He filled his lungs with the cool night air. "If I hadn't been competing in rodeos, I'd probably have gone a little crazy. Bull riding kept my mind off a lot of things."

Her brows knitted together. "You're so good with Ben. I would think you'd want a wife, kids."

"I'm his buddy now. Doesn't have anything to do with parenting." The rodeo and living alone had become his way of life, and Trace was happy.

"But when you talk to Ben, he really listens." She crossed the porch and sat down beside him. "How do you do that? Get him to pay attention?"

Her scent vined around Trace and seemed to lift him up a little.

Beth created magic wherever she went.

He laughed with the exhilaration and need he was feeling.

Beth eased back and smiled. "Oh, you think it's funny I'm asking you for advice. But you do have a way with Ben. He's a lot better since you started mentoring him."

Her sincere gaze pinned him. A new kind of energy flowed through his veins. She was so close that even in the dim light he could see the dark blue nuggets in her eyes.

God, it would be so easy to kiss her again—to hold her and never let her go. But he was the wrong man for her, and they'd promised each other. Beth needed someone who could be a husband and a father. She required a man who was one hundred eighty degrees opposite him.

"I don't know anything about kids, Beth. Don't get the wrong idea about me. I don't have brothers or sisters, and my parents weren't anything to write home about, since we never had a home. Can't understand why the kid likes me."

Beth wet her bottom lip.

A fire inside Trace, already burning, flamed into raging need.

"Ben has told me a little about your conversations, and he showed me the art book you bought him. He loves Remington now."

She laughed, and Trace wondered if he'd ever be able to breathe again.

"I thought the book would encourage him. The kid has talent. Can't see him wasting his time rodeoing when he can do something like that."

Beth sighed. "I know I worry too much. I was so afraid I'd bring him out to Branding and he'd never get the rodeo thing out of his system."

The light from the house danced around her. He blinked and wondered if he wasn't dreaming.

Her sincerity about Ben and her desire to protect him touched Trace the way no other woman had. "He's lucky to have you," he managed to say.

She leaned a little closer. "I'm surprised you'd say that. I'd think the way you feel about the rodeo and the way I feel . . . Well, you just wouldn't say that."

"Not many women would do what you've done. Some would take off. Others, well, they wouldn't work as hard as you do and . . ."

Trace stopped himself. He didn't know what the hell he was talking about. With Beth so close, he wasn't sure about anything except how much he wanted to kiss her sweet lips.

"I have tried to be a good mom. Ray and I were so young when Ben was born. We both made mistakes. We both got hurt because I made decisions with my heart. But I'm not going to do that anymore. Like kissing you the other night . . . I have to think with my head from now on." Her eyes widened as if she was surprised at what she'd just said.

Beth looked so serious, so vulnerable, so beautiful his chest ached, and all he wanted to do was hold her.

"Why don't you stop thinking so much?" he said. Before he could stop himself, his arms swept around her and his lips captured hers.

Trace expected her to resist his embrace, but she didn't. In fact, Beth sighed and almost melted against him, as if she'd been waiting for him to touch her all evening.

When she'd come out to the porch, Beth was sure she wouldn't kiss Trace again. Then, like magic, his words had melted her resolve, and his eyes made her want his sweet lips on hers.

He tilted her head so her mouth fit perfectly on his. Her need vanquished any doubts left, and she moved closer as her body automatically fit with Trace's. She matched each one of his kisses, his tongue flicking hers, his lips soft yet hard.

Beth let her fingers thread through his thick hair and heard herself sigh as need careened through her body like quicksilver.

When his lips left hers, she moaned.

He rained kisses across her cheeks, touched each eyelid with his lips, and then trailed more kisses to her throat. Beth arched in his arms, needing to be closer, to have him touch her where she ached for attention.

Trace groaned. Suddenly he was holding her back by the shoulders and staring into her eyes.

"What?" Automatically she ran the tip of her tongue around her lips, missing his mouth on hers again.

"Beth, I want you," he whispered roughly, his voice laced with need.

She took a deep breath and blinked, realizing what had just happened between them.

Was she losing her mind?

Their promise—her pledge—to stay away from Trace Barlow had evaporated like feathery clouds in the sky. She couldn't let Trace or any cowboy slip into her life again. She wasn't *ever* going through what she had years ago.

Beth pulled away from him. "I shouldn't have let that happen."

His hands were still on her shoulders, his fingers massaging her now tense muscles. Her body was on fire. She'd never kissed a man like that before. She'd never been so out of her mind with need that she didn't know what she was doing and didn't care.

She closed her eyes and forced herself to take a deep breath. If only her heart would stop beating so hard, maybe the craving for Trace to take her in his arms and never let her go would subside.

"Beth," Trace whispered, his voice giving him away. He wanted her as much as she wanted him.

She was afraid if she looked at him, she'd fall right back into his arms. And then what would happen? One more kiss and she wouldn't be able to stop herself. She had to forget these silly emotions.

And the way Trace had whispered her name, she knew his resolve had vaporized, too.

"Beth, are you OK?"

Why did he have to be so concerned? Why couldn't he be like every other cowboy she'd ever known?

She opened her eyes and attached her gaze to his dark one. He was worried about her, and that made it all the harder not to press her body to his.

"Beth?"

"I'm fine. Just disappointed in myself. I never should have let that happen."

He sucked in a large amount of air, held it, then let it out in a whoosh. She connected to his frustration.

"Trace, we both know we shouldn't be out here kissing like a couple of teenagers. I mean, what's the point?"

His sexy half smile cartwheeled its way to her. If she'd been standing, Beth was sure her knees would have given out.

There was something so *sexy* about Trace Barlow. Yet she didn't need or want a man in her life who lived for danger and excitement. She'd made that mistake before.

"I'm not the type of woman who can sleep with you—"

"You think I don't know that? I've never met a woman like you."

She nodded once and fought the urge that was pushing her to wrap her arms around Trace again.

"I have Ben to worry about." She didn't say what else she was thinking. Her heart told her she had other reasons for not falling into his arms.

"I wouldn't expect you to. We'd better draw a line and not cross it. But I won't lie. I'm attracted to you." Trace's lips slid into a grim line. "And I could tell," he said, his brow arching, "you feel the same way."

Heat rose from deep within Beth's belly and slipped over her. There was no denying what she felt.

"Yes, I am. But it doesn't mean—"

"I'll be finished mentoring soon. With Abilene coming up, I won't be around Branding that much anyway."

Beth felt her body stiffen. How could she give her heart to this man? It all boiled down to rodeos and winning. Trace would always have the rodeo in his blood, which meant there was no room for anything or anyone else. And if she let herself care for him, what if something happened to him?

Her heart raced with trepidation.

Beth stood and headed for her front door. Trace put on his hat and left the chair. Even in the dim light, she could see his eyes were still smoky with need for her.

She drew in a breath to steady herself. "I prob-

ably won't see you after this. But I do want to
thank you for what you've done for Ben."

Without thinking she reached out her hand.
His own, warm and callused from roping and riding long hours, encased hers for a moment. The
roughness served to remind her she and Trace
didn't belong together, even if it was for just one
night.

The rodeo owned Trace Barlow heart and soul.

EIGHT

Beth placed the plate in the plastic bus cart and sighed. Waitressing, even in a small cafe, was harder work than she'd ever imagined. She glanced at her watch. Just thirty more minutes and she could go home and check on Ben. She'd called the house a few minutes ago, but Ben hadn't answered.

Ever since Trace had completed his mentoring hours, Ben had been harder to handle. He spent more time in his room or out at the barn. According to his teacher, his grades were dropping again. Ben wouldn't admit it, but Beth knew he missed Trace.

And so did she.

Her heart started to race and she closed her eyes. She wasn't going to start fantasizing about Trace Barlow again.

"Hey, Beth, how are you?"

She turned toward the door. Carol Kelly cut across the small restaurant and sat on a counter stool. The judge was dressed casually in a western shirt and jeans.

"Judge Kelly, it's nice to see you. What can I get for you?"

"I didn't come in to eat."

Beth's stomach sank.

"How are things going for you and Ben?"

"Fine." Beth swallowed hard. She didn't want to tell the judge she was more worried about her son than ever. Besides, she'd make things work out no matter how difficult.

"I talked to Ben's teacher yesterday." Carol folded her hands together on the counter and studied Beth. "Mrs. Wicklyn said Ben's having trouble getting along with his classmates. It started two weeks ago. Is there a problem?"

Beth's heart beat into her throat. Ben had been so much better when Trace was involved in his life. Yet she couldn't expect the man to mentor Ben when he didn't have to, and she didn't want to think of Trace coming back to Oak Creek. She still hadn't settled her feelings, and it would be a long time before she did.

"I've tried talking to Ben," Beth said lamely as her heart pounded out more worry.

"I thought Trace might stick with Ben even though his community service was up, but the man's got his own problems."

"Problems? What problems?" She didn't know why she asked. Trace was probably still searching for land to lease.

Her chest tightened. Oak Creek would be the perfect place for Trace, but the way she felt about the man, she couldn't let him move onto her land. Beth was certain Trace wouldn't, anyway.

"He's going to end up selling his cattle at a loss if he doesn't find a place soon. That's one setback the man does not need. Hurting his leg was one thing, but he's got his hopes on buying back his ranch. I think he really started looking at the place like the home he never had as a kid."

"Trace told me about his ranch," was all she could say. Her mouth was growing dry with this kind of talk.

"Last year he scraped enough money together to buy north of town. Always thought it was good for him to have a place to call home."

"But he's so into rodeos—"

"He never had much of a family. I think the rodeo makes him forget that. When he bought his ranch, he was talking about adding on. Just seemed like what he needed," Carol said.

"Trace was going to add on?"

"Well, you two sure didn't get to know each other very well." Carol pinned her gaze to Beth's. " 'Course, I'm not surprised Trace didn't say anything. He's quiet that way."

Beth's stomach dipped. She and Trace had been too busy kissing and thinking about kissing each other. She took a deep breath. "I'm surprised Trace would want to settle down."

Carol nodded. "He doesn't act like it now, but when he had his own ranch, he wasn't practicing night and day."

"He wasn't?" Beth didn't want to ask, but she couldn't help herself. Trace never got into details about his home or his life before he lost it. This was a Trace she'd never seen.

"When his marriage didn't work out, he was so disappointed. His bull riding kept his mind off things."

"He talked a little bit about his marriage."

Carol arched a brow. "I've known him since he was knee high to a grasshopper. Even when he was a kid, he was quiet. He hasn't said, but if he has to sell his cattle, he's never going to recover financially unless he wins at Abilene. But then he'll probably never get his ranch back."

"Rodeos are so dangerous."

"Sometimes. Trace feels an attachment to the sport because of what it did for him as a kid. It made him feel like he belonged, and it took the place of the family he never had."

There was so much she didn't understand about Trace. Ray Morris had competed for the glory of it. His youth had been so different from what Trace had gone through.

"Now back to Ben. How's he really doing?"

Beth felt her face flush. How in the world had they gotten on the subject of Trace Barlow? Hopefully Carol couldn't see how interested she was in Trace.

"Hey, Beth, phone for you. Something about your kid's in trouble at school," the cook called out from the other side of the room.

Beth's heart rammed at her ribs, then did a

back flip. More trouble with Ben with Carol sitting there. To top everything off, she was feeling all topsy-turvy after talking about Trace for so long.

She glanced at Judge Kelly. Worry lines creased the woman's forehead, and Beth knew this wasn't going to be the perfect ending to a perfect day.

Trace shifted his pickup into neutral and killed the engine. He'd finished rodeo practice an hour ago and decided to come into town. His practice was going well, and he knew he had a good chance of winning big in Abilene.

He stared out the truck windshield at the small feed store. He'd been practicing more and more since he'd quit mentoring Ben. Trace rubbed the side of his leg with his palm. His bones were feeling it, but at least he wasn't thinking about Beth.

His gut tightened at just the vague thought of her, and he wondered how she was doing. Trace clenched his jaw. Even though he could push the woman out of his mind for a little while with rodeo practice, he wouldn't be able to forget her real soon.

"Why, Trace Barlow, just the man I'm looking for."

He glanced to his left. Carol had pulled her utility vehicle up beside his, and he hadn't even heard it.

"Hey, Carol."

He'd been planning on talking to the owner

of the feed store to see if he'd heard of anyone within a fifty-mile radius who was leasing land. Maybe now he'd come back later. But if he didn't find a place in two days, he was going to have to sell his cattle when the market was down and lose big.

He looked back at Carol. Maybe she wouldn't ask a slew of questions about Ben and Beth.

Again Beth's image rose into his mind. He imagined her in the pale light of her front porch, her hair like a halo, her lips soft . . .

Trace gritted his teeth.

He shouldn't be thinking about her, but he couldn't banish the memory of how good she made him feel.

Maybe in a few weeks the need to see Beth Morris would fade a little. He shook his head. That was an impossibility.

Trace forced himself to climb out of his pickup. Carol walked across the gravel and faced him.

"I haven't been speeding, if that's what you're worried about." Trace crossed his arms, but knew that wasn't what Carol wanted to talk to him about.

The judge smiled and cocked an eyebrow. "How's the hunt for the lease going?"

"Terrible." The late afternoon sunshine warmed his back through his cowboy shirt.

"I heard some bad news a while ago."

"Lots of bad news going around lately." He

knew it would be about Beth or Ben, and Trace didn't trust himself to hear it.

"Ben Morris got in a bad fight in school. I've decided to keep him on probation."

Trace's mouth went dry as an old well. "Was he hurt?"

"No, but from what I heard, the principal might suspend him."

"For a fight? Hell, the kid's made progress. Throwing him out of school will only make it worse." His reaction told Trace how much he missed Beth and Ben.

"Yes, that's true. Beth is pretty upset. She left Junior's in a big rush, told the cook she wasn't coming back."

A searing pain attacked his gut. Beth was probably worried out of her mind about her son. And Ben was probably acting moody and giving her a hard time. Beth shouldn't have to go through this all alone. Sure, the kid was a handful, but he wasn't a bad kid. He just needed a guy to relate to.

"If I can't find him another mentor, I'm going to put him on stricter probation." Carol pinned Trace with her gaze.

Trace held up his hands. "Don't get any ideas, Carol. I'm a law-abiding citizen now. That baby," he pointed to his pickup, "hasn't been over fifty in a month."

Carol nodded, then walked around to the driver's side of her own vehicle. "Wouldn't think about you, Trace. You did your duty. I just feel mighty sorry for Beth. She's a nice woman, and I've got the feeling she can't afford to work fewer hours. But with Ben in trouble . . . Well, a person can't be two places at once."

Trace nodded. His body had gone numb, and he stood in the middle of the parking lot. Carol's tires kicked up dust as she headed for the highway.

He felt mighty bad for Beth and Ben, but there was no way he was going to get involved again. He had his own problems to worry about.

"Trace!"

Beth heard Ben yell from the other end of the house. She automatically smoothed her hair and cursed her reaction.

After she'd picked Ben up from school and doctored his scraped knees and puffy lip, she'd sent him to his room to think about the fight he'd gotten into, then yelled down the hall he was on restriction for a month.

She walked into the living room. Why had she said a *month*? How in the world would she survive thirty days with Ben whining and moping around the house?

Ben raced out of his room and ran down the hallway to the living room. "Trace just drove up! Wait till I tell him about the fight."

Beth's mouth went dry. With all her problems, she shouldn't care if Trace Barlow had come to visit—but she did.

His black truck was parked in the drive, and he was just climbing out of the cab. His cowboy hat was angled in its usual way, and he was dressed in a dark blue T-shirt and jeans.

Her hand automatically went to her hair again and she wished she'd run a comb through it. Then she reprimanded herself for caring what she looked like when Trace was around.

It had only been a few days since she'd seen him, but it seemed like a year.

Beth watched him walk toward the house. She hadn't forgotten that special walk he had, the slight limp and the way it made him hold himself a little straighter.

Her gaze drifted to his eyes. They held almost as much worry as she felt.

"Mom, you feeling all right?"

Beth's attention snapped to Ben. "Yes, I'm fine. Just surprised to see Trace out here, that's all."

"Wait till he hears how I flattened that kid." Ben raced out the door and danced around Trace.

The screen door slammed. Beth pushed the door open and walked onto the porch. Her son jumped up and down in front of Trace and then started to tell him the story of what had happened at school.

Since she'd brought him home, all Ben had done was frown and complain. But now that Trace Barlow had arrived, he was a different person.

Trace crossed his arms and looked at Ben.

Beth walked to the edge of the porch and leaned against the railing. Ben was still talking a mile a minute.

"And then I really let him have it. Socked him right in the chin, and his skin split and blood came spurting out, just like in the movies. Coach had to pull us apart. Wow, the guy cried like a baby."

Beth winced and straightened.

"Sounds like a battle. How'd it get started?"

When she'd picked Ben up from school, the principal had told her neither boy would talk about what had caused the fight, and on the way home Ben wouldn't say a word.

"He said my dad wasn't as good as I'm always saying and I should just shut up and quit bragging." Ben tried to jam his scraped fingers in his pockets, but stopped and winced. "Ouch!"

"You hurt your fingers?" Trace seized his wrist and inspected the cuts. His dark eyes couldn't hide his sympathy.

Ben shook him away. "I'm fine. I beat him up for saying that about my dad. I remembered what you said about standing up for things I believe in. So that's what I did." Ben stood straighter.

A huge ache rushed through Beth.

Trace glanced up at her and nodded a hello, then hung his arm around the boy's shoulders. "Your dad was a big rodeo star, Ben. I don't think there'll be a better bull rider for a long time."

With Trace's words, Ben straightened more, squared his shoulders and smiled. "That's what I've been telling everybody at school. I'm not gonna let someone lie about my dad."

What in the world was Trace doing? He didn't need to encourage Ben to hit a classmate. Beth drew in a huge amount of warm air and headed for the steps. She'd stop this immediately. She didn't want his kind of help—or any assistance raising her son. Ben needed to stay out of trouble. But before she could reach them, Trace spoke.

"Ben, anybody who knows the rodeo knows your dad was a big-time star. That kid was just yanking your chain."

Beth nibbled on her bottom lip. The anger that was rising up washed back a little.

Ben's face puckered. "But, Trace, you told me not to say anything I couldn't back up. I kicked that kid's butt for saying what he did. Now I'm gonna work real hard and be a rodeo star myself. I'll show him."

Beth tried to swallow back her gasp, but failed. Trace looked at her for a moment, then back to her son. Thank goodness Ben hadn't heard her. He'd know she was eavesdropping.

Trace knelt so he was eye to eye with Ben. "Son, that kid was just trying to get you going. And he did. Nobody can take your dad's rodeo record away, no matter what anybody says. Even if somebody comes around and beats Ray Morris's title, he was a champ, one of the best. The kid got your goat."

"But, Trace . . ." The pride fell from Ben's face. "Aren't you proud of me?"

Beth's entire body throbbed for her son and her heart melted for Trace. Why did he always know the right words to say to Ben? And why couldn't she do the same thing?

"I'm always proud of you. But you don't need to fight for your dad's memory. He was a star. Don't you let anybody get you in trouble when they say different."

Trace patted Ben's shoulder. "And about this rodeoing . . . you shouldn't give up your artwork and your talent. You know how many cowboys would like to be able to draw and paint like you do instead of beating their brains out on a horse or a bull?"

Ben hung his head toward the dusty gravel drive and kicked at the stones. "Aw, I'm not that good."

"Yes, you are. But I ran into Judge Kelly and she told me if you don't shape up in school, she's gonna put you on a stricter probation."

Beth's heart caught in her throat again. So that's where Trace had heard about Ben. If the court was brought back into Ben's life, Beth wasn't sure what he'd do.

Ben kicked at another pebble and dust rose around him and Trace. "Guess I screwed up, huh?"

"Every man screws up, buddy. You just gotta

keep on learning." Trace gripped Ben by the shoulders and pushed him back a little. "Look at that lip. You look like that rock star, what's-his-name. The one with the Rolling Stones."

"Mick Jagger is so old he needs a wheelchair."

"Yeah, but he can sing." Trace's hand brushed back Ben's hair and whistled. "And you're gonna have some kind of a shiner." He patted Ben on the shoulder again and then his gaze connected with Beth's.

Trace's dark eyes looked velvety and kind even in the harsh sunlight. The man had talked to her son so easily, convinced him he didn't need to fight anymore.

"I bet your mama put you on restriction, big time." Trace's attention stayed fixed on Beth.

Her stomach flip-flopped like a teenager's.

"Yeah, I've gotta stay in my room two days. I can't watch any TV for a month. Plus she cut her hours back at Junior's. Now she'll be around a lot more."

"You better head on back to your jail cell, then," Trace stood, yet didn't take his eyes off Beth. "Maybe we can get you off for good behavior."

Ben ran to the porch, hopped up the stairs, and let the screen door slam shut. Beth held very still and tried to get her heartbeat back to normal.

Trace crossed the drive and stopped at the bottom of the steps. His gaze met hers again.

"Hey," he said, his voice low. "Are you OK?"

She heard the distress laced through his simple question.

"Hey, yourself." Beth patted the wayward strands of hair back into her braid, then crossed her arms. "Obviously you ran into Carol."

"I think she came looking for me."

"Thanks for coming out and talking to him." He'd done a better job with Ben and she knew it. It hurt. Ben was her responsibility, not anyone else's.

"I wanted to talk to Ben and . . ."

"And what?"

"And nothing." Trace shook his head, then stared at her. "That's not true. I was worried about you, mostly. I was the one who told him he needed to back up anything he said. I wanted to make sure he didn't confuse it with fighting, and I didn't think it was fair to leave you with the problem."

The last thing Beth wanted was for Trace Barlow to worry about her. "Ben doesn't need to hear about what a hero Ray Morris was. He'll want to be just like him."

"I didn't say he was a hero. The man was good at what he did, and that kid in there," Trace nodded toward the house, "needs to know that. I'm not much on kids, but I don't think it would do him any good to deny what his old man accomplished when he was living."

Beth's throat hurt so much she couldn't swallow or speak for a moment. Fear surrounded her. How could she lose anyone else she loved?

"Beth, I didn't mean to interfere."

"I know. It's just—I can't let Ben be in any kind of danger."

"Ben's gonna think and talk about his father. If you try to stop him, it'll only make it worse. My old man wasn't the best, but I think about him, still care about him."

Trace was right. God, she didn't want to admit it, though. If she could just wipe Ray Morris's memory out of Ben's mind like chalk from a blackboard, she'd do it. Yet that wasn't a good idea, either. Ben needed something to hang on to.

Tears threatened, but Beth blinked them away. She wouldn't give in to tears right now. She crossed to the chair and sat. Drawing in a deep breath, she rubbed her forehead with her fingertips.

"Beth." He climbed the stairs and crossed the porch. "Are you OK? I know you must be worried about Ben."

She shook her head because she couldn't speak. If she did, she knew she'd cry, and that was the last thing she wanted to do right now. A long time ago she'd made up her mind she'd be both parents to Ben, and she wasn't giving up now.

"Hey, Ben's gonna be OK. Boys that age fight. Happens all the time. You're doing a fine job raising him."

Trace wrapped his arm around her shoulders and his warmth drifted through her body.

The tears that were threatening moved closer to the surface and she sniffed. "I know I can raise Ben, but I always wonder if I'm doing what I should. I can't leave him alone, not with Carol worried about him, and he's talking about the rodeo again. I cut back my hours at Junior's, which means we won't have a lot of money."

She brushed at the corner of her eyes. She shouldn't be telling Trace her problems. He had his own mess to contend with.

"Yeah, money. It's pretty much a pain in the neck when you don't have any. When you've got a lot of cash, everything is Jim Dandy."

Trace's eyes held that certain sparkle that was unique to him. She laughed and shook her head. "Lots of money can cause problems, too." Ray had been too young to have so much money, and he'd blown it all.

"True, but there's got to be a happy medium."

She managed a tiny laugh through her tears. The man could make her feel she was dancing on air even when she was so worried. "Maybe I should go back to Dallas."

Wrinkles shadowed his forehead. "That's not gonna help. You'd still have to work, and Ben might get in with the same old crowd."

He was right. Dallas wasn't the answer. She wasn't thinking straight. "Talk about a rock and a hard spot. Carol is going to put Ben on a stricter probation again if I don't find another mentor."

Trace nodded and a muscle twitched in his

jaw. "Yeah, he needs a mentor. Maybe we can fix the mentor problem, your money problems, and my land problems all at once."

NINE

Damn!

Why had he said anything at all?

Because Beth was looking at him with her baby blues, and he'd never be able to leave her with so much trouble on her hands. He realized there wasn't too much he could refuse when it came to Beth Morris.

"That's a big *idea,*" was all she said.

"Why don't you let me put my cattle on your land and rent the upstairs room in the barn?" Trace said the words fast so he didn't have time to take any of it back.

Beth's eyes widened and she blinked. "I don't think so, Trace."

"Hey." He stood and crossed the porch so he'd be far enough away from her. "Before you say no, give yourself time to think about my idea. It's the only way to solve everybody's problems."

She stared at him in disbelief. "And how would that solve *everyone's* problems? Seems to me your being here would cause more dilemmas for both of us."

He could see the apprehension in her gaze and knew what she was thinking. It would be impossible for them to be so close and not respond.

Hell, he and Beth needed miles between them. Even that didn't keep him from dreaming about her.

But she needed help, and he wasn't about to let her down. He cleared his throat and forced himself to speak. "I'm worried about Ben. Carol told me he was doing better when I was mentoring him."

Beth nodded. "He was."

"And you need money. I'll pay you a good sum to rent your land. That way you won't have to work so much, and I'll be close to help out."

At his last words, she stiffened. "That's not such a good idea. Did you forget what happened?"

"How could I?" Trace leaned against the banister. He'd been drowning with thoughts of Beth.

"Well then, you should realize your moving out here just won't work."

"We have to make it work for Ben's sake. Carol was serious about the probation extension, and you can't work fewer hours."

"I know." Beth stared at him. "And you need a place, don't you?"

"Yeah, in two days. But believe me, that's not why I'm offering to do it. We've got to think about Ben. I care about the kid, and I don't want him to go bad. It's real easy at that age."

"I know," Beth whispered.

"It'll just be for a few weeks. When I win the prize money I'm counting on, I'll have my own place back and by then Ben will have settled down."

"A few weeks? A lot can happen in a few *days.*"

Although her tone was sarcastic, Trace could tell she was thinking about letting him move out to Oak Creek.

Suddenly anxiety filled her gaze. Then she stood. All he wanted to do was wrap his arms around her and tell her not to worry.

But he held back. He didn't want to cause Beth any more problems. At the moment, they needed each other for other reasons, and he wanted to help her. "Just think about it, Beth."

She took a deep breath and bit her bottom lip. "You won't talk about rodeos, and you'll encourage Ben to paint?"

"Yeah, like I did before. He listens to me."

She closed her eyes for a moment and her chest rose. Then she looked at him, her face a vision of innocence. "It's the only way. We . . . Well, it's not going to be . . ." She hesitated, closed her eyes again, and took another deep, agitated breath.

Her softly rounded breasts pressed against her T-shirt, and Trace could see the faint outline of her nipples. His jeans grew tighter. Staying away from Beth was going to be almost impossible, but he'd do it.

She opened her eyes and looked at him hard for a moment. "Your coming to live here really is the only way, isn't it?" Her voice was barely a whisper.

"It is. With all I have to do, you probably won't even see me."

"Right!" She laughed.

She had one lovely laugh. Hell, Beth Morris had one lovely everything, but she was right. Living so close, it would be difficult not to get tangled up.

"I'll stay out of your way, Beth. I don't need to get involved right now."

She nodded but didn't smile. "I'll go get you the key to the room in the barn."

"It's locked?"

She turned back and arched a delicate brow. "Trace, everything is locked around here, and it's going to stay that way."

He met her gaze. Trace Barlow knew exactly what Beth was talking about.

Beth sighed, sat on the couch, and smoothed the skirt of the dress she'd put on after her shower. Why couldn't she stop thinking about Trace? He was on her mind all the time now that he'd moved to Oak Creek.

At night when she tried to go to sleep, he invaded her dreams, kissing her and making love to her. In the morning, she was exhausted.

Yet her son had been doing much better since Trace had moved himself and his cattle out to the ranch. Ben, of course, had his grouchy moments, but with the cowboy around, the ten-year-old's problems at school had eased, and he'd quit bugging her about riding horses and roping.

Beth was more worried about herself than anything. Even though they'd vowed to keep their distance, in the last few days she and Trace had run into each other constantly. They were cordial—Trace would nod or tip his hat, and her stomach would take a nosedive toward the earth.

The man was just impossible to forget.

He'd kept his promise about not influencing Ben about rodeos. Trace practiced somewhere other than Oak Creek.

Beth shook her head to rid her mind of the useless thoughts. She didn't care what Trace did with his life as long as he didn't talk to Ben about it.

However, she couldn't deny her respect for the man had grown. Ben was happy, and that was all that mattered. Beth ran her fingers through her freshly washed hair. Last night when she'd leaned over Ben's bed and told him good night, he'd sat up and babbled something about a surprise he'd planned for her late this afternoon.

She'd almost forgotten today was her birthday. She was so used to not celebrating her own birthday it seemed strange to get ready for the event. But she didn't want to disappoint Ben, so she'd put on the pretty blue summer dress and white sandals he'd helped her pick out this morning.

She peeked out the front window to the barn, where Ben had headed three hours ago. Her son was running up the path to the house. Suddenly she heard him thump onto the porch steps.

"M-o-o-o-m, you ready?"

She met him at the door. His hair gleamed with sunshine and he smelled like freshly washed clothes that had been hanging on the line all afternoon.

Ben would be out of school soon for the summer and the days would be Texas hot. With some of the money Trace had given her a few days ago, she'd paid for a week of summer art camp for Ben.

The principal had told her about the Houston camp that catered to young people who were artistically talented. She hadn't told Ben about it yet. Tomorrow she'd surprise him with the gift.

Ben smiled up at her. "Are you ready for your birthday *surprise*? Bet you aren't even gonna believe your present." He bobbed up and down, excitement brimming out of him.

A smile opened his lips, and Beth's heart sang. It felt so good to see her son happy, not moody and wishing he was somewhere else.

"Mom, I've got it all planned out. We're going to the barn first, and then I've got another surprise!" Ben leaped off the porch and ran backward for a moment. "Come on, Mom!"

Beth hesitated for a moment. Trace's truck was parked in his usual spot next to the barn. He must have finished his practice early. She didn't want to run into him, but she wasn't about to disappoint Ben, either.

"Mom, come on. Why are you just standing there?"

Laughing, she sprinted toward her son. Ben giggled and ran across the field, his blond hair flapping. Then he disappeared around the corner of the barn.

She slowed when she came to the barn. Trace had promised he'd work on the place, and he'd kept his word. Most of the fences were mended, and there was no telling what else the man had done. He was either working, practicing, or spending time with her son.

Ben ran out of the barn door. "Did you see the fences?" He pointed to the area she'd just inspected. "I helped Trace. He showed me how to fix them. Next week he's gonna let me paint again."

"That's great," Beth managed. "They look really nice."

"But those aren't your surprises. Come on." He seized her hand and pulled her inside the barn. "In here."

Beth's attention jumped around the barn. Trace wasn't in sight, and her pulse calmed a little.

She was just being silly.

He was probably resting in his room, and they wouldn't even see each other.

Relaxed, she let her attention return to the barn again. Trace had made some improvements on the inside, too.

"Mom, come on. Don't you want to see your surprise?"

She followed a galloping Ben down to his art room. He flung open the door. When Beth entered, he was standing with his arms crossed, a huge smile gracing his face.

An image of herself stared back. She could easily see it was the best work Ben had ever done.

"It's beautiful." She crossed the room to hug Ben and ruffle his hair. "This is the best . . . birthday . . . Well, I'm so surprised." And she was, too. She hadn't expected Ben to paint her portrait.

Ben pushed away from her and crossed his arms again. "Aw, geez, Mom, don't start crying. And quit hugging me."

Beth laughed and sniffed back her tears, then dabbed the outside corners of her eyes with the back of her hand. "I can cry if I want to. It's my birthday."

"*Happy birthday!* Do you like it, really?"

She stepped closer to the painting. It was so wonderful, and surrounding the edge was a simple oak frame. She ran her thumb over the smooth wood. "Where in the world did you get this? It's lovely."

"Trace made it. Says he's going to show me how to make frames for all my work."

Beth's heart thumped out of control again. Why in the world did the man have to be so . . . so thoughtful?

"The painting is ready for hanging. Trace put

a wire on the back." Ben turned it around, showing her the screws and the thin cable.

"I love my present. It's perfect. I know exactly where I'm going to hang it." She hugged him again. "I love it because you painted it."

"This isn't all." He put his hands on his hips and smiled like a cat.

"More? Why, honey, this is enough."

Ben squared his shoulders. Since Trace had moved to Oak Creek her son's self-confidence had grown. "No, it isn't. I've planned a party."

"A party?"

"Yep. I didn't tell you, but I've been saving my allowance. I'm taking you to the pizza parlor in Branding. They've got video games!"

Ben ran out of the room and Beth followed. When she reached him, he was yelling up to Trace's room.

"Ben, don't bother Trace."

"I want him to come, too."

Trace walked out of his room and smiled. "Hey, buddy." Immediately Trace's eyes were on her, and heat from deep in her belly expanded out to her extremities. He had on a black T-shirt that announced the Abilene Rodeo Finals and accented his dark hair and eyes. As he drew closer, she could see the hair at his nape was still damp from his shower.

Handsome wasn't a good enough word for the man.

"Hi, Beth," he said, his voice low. "Happy birthday."

The two words, the way he said them, almost made her knees buckle. But she pushed back the feelings. His scent—Old Spice, she was sure—wound around her, and her mouth turned dry.

"Mom, you OK? You've got that weird look on your face again."

Beth heard herself giggle. When she was around Trace she felt like a young girl. "Oh, Ben, don't be silly."

"Hey, Trace, you've got to go to the pizza parlor with us for Mom's birthday."

Without shifting his gaze from Beth, Trace shook his head. "No, you two go on ahead. It's a family party."

"I saved enough for all three of us to go. If you don't come, you'll ruin Mom's birthday." Ben crossed his arms.

"Ben, maybe Trace is really busy," Beth said.

"It's your birthday. He's gotta come along, or he'll ruin the party." Ben's voice was laced with disappointment.

Trace cleared his throat. "I don't want to—"

"Ben, the two of us will have a good time, and I'm sure Trace has better things to do."

"But it's not even a party with two. I've been saving and planning." Disappointment filled her son's gaze. "Please, Trace, come with us. Mom's always happy around you."

"Ben, maybe Trace—"

"It's OK, Beth. I have time."

"See, Mom, he wants to. Yahoo!" Ben yelled

as he headed for the barn door. "Let's go in Trace's truck. I get shotgun!"

Beth looked at Trace and tried to smile. His attention had never left her, and her skin heated. "You don't have to drive," she said. "I can do that."

With Ben sitting by the window, she'd have to sit in the middle—too close to Trace. "In fact, you don't even have to go if you really don't want to. I'm not sure how good the pizza will be."

Trace shifted. Then the corners of his mouth curved up. "I wouldn't want to disappoint him by changing his plans. I'll go. Besides, who can ruin pizza?"

Seeing his smile, Beth had to acknowledge how much she'd missed just talking to Trace. Even though it had only been a few days since they'd spoken, it seemed like an eternity.

She couldn't let herself start thinking this way. She didn't *need* to miss Trace Barlow. She needed to forget him.

Trace climbed in next to Beth and gritted his teeth. Her warmth and sweet scent enveloped him. For the last few days, he'd managed not to think about her every minute of the day—just every hour or so.

"Put the pedal to the metal, Trace. But don't speed," Ben cried excitedly.

The kid was something else.

"OK," he said, hoping he could dispel the disruption growing inside of him. Beth was staring straight ahead, keeping herself as far away from him as she could in the tight confines of his pickup's bench seat.

"I've got plenty of money." Ben waved a wad of dollar bills at them, then lifted his hip and stuffed it back in his pocket. The quick motion shifted Beth toward Trace, the soft curve of her breast pressing against his biceps.

Molten need splashed through his body and took his good sense away.

"Sorry," she whispered, her gaze meeting his for a moment.

Trace let himself look at her a moment too long. Her soft blond hair framed her face gently and emphasized her blue eyes more. The summer dress she'd chosen to wear accented her beauty, and Trace knew he'd never seen a lovelier woman than Beth.

She turned toward Ben, rubbed his shoulder, and kissed his cheek. "Thank you for my present, honey."

"Aw, M-o-o-o-m. Come on, Trace, let's go."

Trace started his pickup. As they traveled along in silence, Trace gambled another glance toward his passengers. Beth still had her arm around Ben and they looked happy, the way a mother and son should.

And Beth—she took his breath away, but it wasn't just her beauty that had stolen his heart. Beth hadn't wanted him to come along, but for her son's sake, she was making the best of the situation—as any mom who loved her kid would do. And she'd let him move out to Oak Creek because of Ben.

Even though he didn't understand anything about family life or this kind of devotion, his admiration for Beth had grown by leaps and bounds.

She was the kind of woman any man would admire and never be able to forget, but he had to. Beth didn't need him. She'd made that perfectly clear. And she was right. He wasn't the man who could make her happy and build a family with her.

Trace swallowed hard. No matter how difficult it was going to be, he had to remember they didn't belong together.

TEN

Beth kept her attention on her father's ranch house as Trace cut the engine to his truck. The night surrounded them, and the dim light from the house only accented the country darkness.

Ben opened the passenger door and jumped out. Beth immediately scooted over. All the way home from the pizza parlor, she'd been so aware of Trace's body next to hers that her muscles were now aching.

"Did you have the best time *ever*, Mom?"

Beth laughed at Ben's never-ending enthusiasm. "Yes, the best time *ever*." She hopped from the truck and walked around it as Ben bounced in front of her.

Trace was standing next to the hood with his arms crossed.

She drew Ben into her arms and hugged him. "Thank you, honey, thank you so much. I had a wonderful time. It was a mom's dream birthday. But it's getting late. You still have school tomorrow."

Ben hugged her back, then pulled away. "You

forgot to bring your portrait up to the house. I'll go get it."

Before Ben could head for the barn, Beth put her hand on his shoulder to stop him.

"You need to go to bed." If she let Ben traipse down to the barn for her gift, there was no telling when he'd get to bed, and lack of sleep made her son one cranky boy.

"You don't like my gift." Ben crossed his arms like Trace and stared at his mother.

"Ben, that's not so. I love it. I just forgot to get it from the barn."

"If you liked it, you'd want it in the house."

"Ben, I love it."

"Then I'll go get it for you," Ben said.

"No! Right after you go to bed, I'll go down to the barn, and we'll hang it together *tomorrow.*"

Ben looked at his mother, then smiled. "It is your birthday. So for one more present I'll go to bed, no arguments."

Beth laughed, then threw him the key. Ben galloped for the house. When he reached the door he turned. "Go on, Mom. I promise, I'll go straight to bed. Trace, will you drive her and make sure she gets back OK?"

Beth and Trace laughed at the same time. Ben opened the screen door and let it slap shut.

"If only I could teach him not to slam doors, I'd feel I'd made some progress."

Trace chuckled again, and Beth turned toward him. They were standing three feet apart.

"Don't sell yourself short. You've taught him

a lot of good things. Slamming doors isn't a real big part of life."

Beth smiled. "Thanks." They'd had an incredibly good time tonight. To anyone who didn't know them, they must have looked like the perfect family—mother, father, and son—and that knowledge scared her.

"You don't have to drive me down to the barn. I can walk. The exercise will do me good," she said.

"I'm going that way. You haven't forgotten I live there, have you?" He walked around to the passenger side of his truck and opened the door.

She laughed instead of saying what she was thinking. How in the world could she forget Trace was only a few hundred feet away from her when she climbed into her lonely bed?

As soon as they arrived at the barn, Trace was out of the truck and around the side to open her door before she had time to do it herself.

"I'll walk you back up to the house as soon as you're ready," he said when they entered Ben's art room.

"That's not necessary, Trace."

"I have to." Trace stood by the door as she crossed the room and picked up her painting.

"You have to?" Beth turned back around.

Trace took off his hat and smoothed his hair back as he always did.

"Yeah, I promised Ben. He asked me to make sure you get home all right. He wouldn't think much of me if I didn't keep my word."

His voice was lower than usual, and when he winked, her stomach plummeted.

"Ben admires you. And I know he trusts you." She had so many things to thank the man for she wasn't sure where to start, or if she could stop once she started.

Beth picked up her present and rubbed the frame with the tips of her fingers. "It was nice of you to make this. Ben told me you're going to show him how to make them."

"Yeah, I enjoyed it. Worked on the wood at night when I couldn't sleep."

Her heart picked up its pace. So Trace was having trouble sleeping, too. She drew in a deep breath to settle herself. She had a son to raise and worry about. She didn't have time for any frivolous thinking.

"I should just write out a list of thank yous," she forced herself to say, even though her heart was beating into her throat now.

"I don't need any thanks."

"But you do. Since you moved to Oak Creek, he's doing so much better in school. You even loaned Ben money tonight when he ran out."

Trace lifted his dark brow. "So you saw that move? And here I thought I was being pretty slick."

Beth couldn't help but smile. After they'd gotten to the pizza parlor, Ben had gone off to play the video games and she and Trace had talked easily. When the pizza was served, Trace had passed him some folded bills inconspicuously.

"Yes. It was very nice of you."

"Hey, I've been there—spent too much money in front of a lady. Except I didn't have anyone to bail me out. Ben deserves a little boost."

"Carol told me you practically raised yourself," she said before she could stop herself. Trace wasn't the type of man who would want his past talked about.

Trace's dark eyes narrowed, but he smiled a little. "I didn't have it all that bad. The rodeo made my life worth living. The prize money helped out a lot, too."

Beth's heart ached as she thought of Trace as a kid, without anyone to care for him. "Let me pay you back," she offered again and placed her painting against the wall. She pulled out some extra cash she'd put in her pocket this afternoon and stepped toward Trace.

"No way! It wasn't all that much." Trace held up his hand.

"Really, Trace." Beth stepped closer and tried to slip the folded bills into his shirt pocket.

Trace gently seized her wrist and laughed. "Hey, it was my pleasure."

The pad of his thumb massaged the inside of her wrist, and his heat tore through her body. With the surprise of Trace's touch, Beth lost her balance, and she had to rest her free hand against his chest.

Trace's heart beat erratically against her palm.

She drew in a breath and his scent surrounded her as their gazes connected.

"I wish you would take . . ." She leaned back a little to give herself some space from him.

"I wanted to help Ben." He plucked the money out of her hand and slipped it back into her own pocket, his fingers lightly touching her hip. "Come on, I'll walk you home."

His words brought her out of her daze. Trace was right. She needed to get back to the house so she could make sure Ben had gone to bed.

But more than anything, she needed to put some distance between them.

Trace leaned against the porch railing and sucked in more air. His heart was still imitating a stampede. If he knew what was good for him, he'd walk down the porch steps and across the field to his room . . . *now.* But before he could leave, Beth walked out onto the porch.

"He's sound asleep. The video games must have worn him out."

She was standing between him and the open door. The faint light from the living room surrounded her, accenting her curves.

His mind conjured an image of Beth without any clothes, her body lighted only by a dim lamp, her skin shining like porcelain.

His entire body ached to hold her. "Yeah," was all he could say.

"You sound tired. I'm sorry we kept you out so late. Can I offer you a beer? It's the least I can do since you won't let me pay you for Ben's loan."

Trace wasn't tired at all. No, when he was around Beth, he felt like he could rope three steers in record time. "Nah, I'm fine. Just enjoying the end of the evening. Forget the money. I'm getting a bargain with the room and the land."

She sat in her usual chair and crossed her legs at the ankles. "Are the room and bath working out all right?"

He nodded. The only trouble he had was getting to sleep at night. He felt like a push-pull toy he'd seen once in a Wal-Mart. All he wanted was to be with Beth, but for her sake, he needed to keep his distance.

She glanced down at her wristwatch. "My birthday's almost over. I guess it's back to reality for this Cinderella." Her voice was just above a whisper.

"You look like a princess."

She stared at him for a moment, then shook her head and laughed. "Why, thank you. It was nice of you to join us."

"I liked tonight. It was fun." He'd had a great time and couldn't imagine wanting to be anywhere else.

She crossed her arms and stared out at the night sky.

"Are you cold?"

"No. It's very pleasant tonight. I love Texas at this time of year, when it's not too hot."

"You've always lived in Texas?"

Beth turned a little. "Yes, small towns in the Texas panhandle when I was a kid. After Ray had his accident, I moved to Dallas."

"You wanted to live in the big city?"

She laughed gently. "Not at all. I could make more money in Dallas, and that was better for Ben. And after Ray . . . Well, I needed a change. How about you?"

"Always lived in Branding."

"And your ex-wife?"

"She moved to Houston after we broke up."

"Do you ever see her?"

"No. She pretty much got her fill of rodeos when she was married to me. She never understood." Trace took a deep breath. Beth was so easy to talk to. "The rodeo really saved me when I was a kid. Made me feel like I belonged to something." He looked at Beth again. She was really listening to him. "And when I win Abilene, I'm going to buy my ranch back."

"How'd you lose it in the first place?" She wasn't just making conversation. Beth seemed to want to know.

"Last year when I busted my leg in three places, things just went to hell from there."

"Is that why you limp?"

Trace nodded.

"Aren't you afraid it'll happen again?"

"That's why I switched to roping. No chance of any more accidents. Besides, age isn't on my side anymore."

Beth gulped in the night air and sighed. "There are *always* accidents."

From the way she said the words, Trace knew she'd lived with her fear for a long time.

"You must miss your ranch," Beth finally said.

"Yeah. It's north of town. First real home I ever had."

She turned a little. Her concerned, sparkling blue eyes caught his gaze, and his heart pumped hard. "Where'd you live before?"

"Rented places or rooms. When I was married, we rented a pretty little house near town. Before that, my old man and I flopped where we could. Always had a dream of owning a house with some land attached to it."

"It sounds like you want roots."

"Wouldn't call what I need roots. My botched marriage proved to me I'm no good at the family thing or commitment." Trace felt his chest tighten. He came from people who were loners, and he couldn't change history. "Besides, I figure the way I am, I can't have rodeos and a family, and I'm not about to give up the rodeo."

"But you were young when your marriage broke up, weren't you?" Beth was still facing him.

"All of nineteen. Didn't know marriage involved sticking to something when the going got rough. Rodeo was in my blood by then, and—well, I don't need to explain to you. You lived the same story."

Her delicate brows knitted for a moment as

she studied him. "But you used the rodeo to exist, to take care of yourself."

Trace didn't want Beth to think he was different from any other rodeo bum. She was the kind of woman who was ever hopeful. Once tied to someone, she would never give up on a man. And he was just the opposite, not capable of meeting an obligation for any length of time.

"I'm not any different than any other cowboy." The words came out flat, just the way he wanted them to.

She stood. Her hands found the curve of her hips and she rested them there. The light from the house surrounded her like a halo.

When his attention came back to her face, she pinned him with her blue eyes.

"At times . . . like now, you . . . seem so *different,"* she said, her voice husky. Her breath was coming faster and her chest rose and fell in a steady rhythm.

Without thinking, Trace left his chair and found himself standing next to her. Her perfume, sweet and charming, enveloped him, drawing him closer. He knew, deep down, he had to tell her.

"I'm not different, Beth. Believe me, I'm not. I'm a loner. I've never been able to commit to anyone or anything. I learned that when my marriage busted up—even before that. I don't know anything about keeping a family together or *forever."*

She turned toward him and opened her eyes

just a little bit wider. He took a deep breath and suddenly his arms were around her.

Without another thought, Trace crushed Beth to his chest, his lips finding hers.

Beth clung to Trace and combed her fingers through his hair. He turned her head gently to slant her mouth so it matched his own. His tongue plunged into her moist, waiting mouth, and she sighed.

God, how she loved the taste of him, his touch, his now-familiar aroma. She matched each move he made, letting her tongue dance with his. When his hands trailed over her body, he pulled her closer so she could feel his raging manhood. She arched up and pressed herself against him.

He groaned and strung kisses from her mouth to her cheek, then downward to the indention at the base of her throat.

His fiery lips on her sensitive skin fanned the flames deep within her, and she leaned back in his arms and moaned.

Suddenly his mouth was on hers again, his tongue urging her on, his hands bringing her more alive.

For so long she'd just been moving through life—until Trace had come along and awakened feelings she'd forgotten.

His lips were next to her ear and his quick

breath feathered against her skin. "Beth, I want you. Let's go inside."

Trace's hand trailed to her breast and he touched her peaked nipple.

She kissed him hard, wanting to encourage him. How could she let this heaven end? She leaned back a little in his arms, and he took advantage of the move as his head dipped and found the curve of her breast. He tugged at the top of her dress a little and his tongue painted circles against her bare skin.

Beth moaned as his fingers circled her taut nipple.

"I want you," Trace growled. He picked her up, cradled her in his arms, and headed for the door.

The swift movement startled Beth and she opened her eyes.

Good Lord, what was she doing?

Her thoughts plunged back to earth and she pressed her hands against Trace's heaving chest. "Stop!"

He kissed her lips and brought her closer to him.

"We have to stop. This won't work," she breathed.

Trace closed his eyes and groaned. Beth could feel his heart thumping against her hand.

"Put me down," she managed to whisper.

His arms tightened around her.

"Trace, you have to let me go."

He gently released her and she stood carefully,

wondering if her legs would hold her or if she'd fall in a heap. Her body was still humming with need for Trace's embrace, his kiss, his touch.

She adjusted her dress. What in the world had she been thinking—or *not* thinking—when she'd let this go too far?

Her gaze shifted to Trace, and she answered her own question. Trace Barlow made her feel like a woman. No man had ever done that. With just a kiss or a stroke of his fingers, she was his and he was hers, and nothing else mattered.

"You'd better go in, or I'm not sure what's going to happen next," he said, his voice laced with frustration.

Her mouth turned to dust. There was no doubt he wanted her as much as she needed him.

His chin dipped down, and he studied his cowboy boots for a moment. Then he looked up, his dark eyes narrowed and velvety. "I wasn't planning on stopping."

"I wasn't either." She stepped back a little and hugged herself to keep from touching him. "We can't let this go any farther. We're too different. You love the rodeo and I hate what it did to my life. I don't have room for . . . *this.*"

His brows knitted together and she wasn't sure he understood. But how could she make love to Trace and not get involved?

She'd never been able to divide herself between love and sex.

"Beth, you don't have to explain. I know I'm

not the right guy for you." His dark eyes grew more serious.

Her heart pounded so hard it almost choked her. "Trace, it *can't* happen again." Beth knew with all her heart if they kissed again, she wouldn't be able to stop. "It can't."

Trace nodded once and crossed the porch. Without looking back, he marched down the steps and disappeared into the darkness.

Beth wouldn't let herself move. She was afraid if she did, she'd run after Trace and beg him to take her back in his arms and drown her with kisses.

The crisp night air swirled around her. Maybe someday she'd forget what it felt like when Trace held her, but it wouldn't be soon.

Why had she fallen into his arms so easily? Beth shook her head. It didn't matter why.

She closed her eyes and pushed back the dreaded thoughts. She had to be extra strong on this one. She couldn't bring Trace so close. Her son had suffered enough from losing Ray and not having his father around. So had she, and she wasn't about to let them be hurt again.

She'd loved Ray Morris long ago without thinking of the consequences, and where had that gotten her?

Alone and without many memories to savor.

Trace had told her flat-out he didn't know how to make a commitment. Her judgment about men was getting worse. Her fingertips found her lips and muffled the gasp falling from them.

How could she even think about loving Trace?

ELEVEN

Trace took the last nail out of his mouth and held it against the board. Rodeo practice today had gone great. He'd worked extra hard. The feeling everything was going to be OK surrounded him, as it always did when he was getting ready to compete.

And to make his life even better, a couple of guys had stopped by and announced Trace was a shoo-in for winning at Abilene.

He expanded his lungs. They were right. Taking the roping championship at Abilene would be a cinch, and he felt great despite the other night. Even with all the work he'd been doing, he couldn't stop thinking about Beth.

Trace slammed the nail into the board. This was one of the last fences around the barn that needed repairing. He'd start on the ones in the pastures tomorrow. If he kept himself busy enough, maybe Beth wouldn't fill most of his thoughts.

It can't happen again.

Her words had haunted him when he'd tried

to sleep. They'd reinforced the fact he wasn't cut out to be with Beth. She needed promises of tomorrows, a world filled with family and happiness.

He should be happy she'd stopped him, but he wasn't. Hell, his body ached for the woman, and not just physically, either. He liked being around Beth, no matter what they were doing.

Thank God Beth had enough sense to stop. He sure hadn't. He'd been so turned on by her, he didn't know up from down.

Trace hammered the nail again and swore. As soon as he won Abilene, he'd get himself far away from Beth—for her sake. By then Ben would be OK. Maybe Carol could find someone else to take over the mentoring job.

"Come back here! We are not finished discussing this matter."

Trace watched as Ben bolted across the field toward the barn. Beth, in her customary T-shirt, shorts, and tennis shoes, ran after him. Her ponytail lifted and fell with each move.

Trace drew in a breath, remembering how it had felt to kiss her and hold her.

God, he could almost hear her breathing softly in his ear.

"Ben, stop this minute!" Beth yelled.

"I'm not going," Ben screamed over his shoulder. He stopped by the fence Trace had just repaired and climbed it. "I don't give a darn what you say."

Trace hesitated for a moment, not wanting to

interfere, but he made the mistake of looking at Beth, twenty feet away. Her pretty face was covered with worry; her blue eyes had lost their usual sparkle.

"Hey, kid, calm down." Trace stepped toward Ben. "Don't talk to your mama that way."

"She didn't even ask me. She treats me like a baby all the time. I hate her."

"Whoa, Ben, watch your mouth." Trace put down the hammer and glared at him.

"I told you to come back to the house," Beth said firmly when she got to the fence.

As always, she looked as pretty as a picture, even with the worry clouding her eyes. Trace gritted his teeth. Right now all he wanted to do was hold her and make her feel better.

"I'm not coming back to the house. I'm moving to the barn with Trace!" Ben climbed the last rung of the fence and hopped over to the other side.

Beth bit her bottom lip and glared at her son.

"What's going on? Quiet down or you'll upset my cattle."

Beth shifted her attention to Trace, her lips parted in surprise. "Disturb your cattle? What are you talking about?"

Trace's gut tightened. There was no way he'd ever forget this woman. He squared his jaw and reminded himself he had to.

Ben laughed loudly. "Yeah, Mom, quit yelling at me. You're gonna cause more trouble. You're always doing that."

"Ben!" The fire in her eyes blazed again.

Trace had to shift his attention to Ben to fight the overwhelming need to comfort Beth. "Ben, that's no way to talk to your mama." He didn't want to get mixed up in the family argument, but he wasn't going to let anyone talk to Beth that way. Besides, when the kid grew up he'd regret his words.

"You don't know what she did," Ben whined. He stared at Trace. "She treats me like a big baby."

"If you want to be grown up, start by not talking to your mama that way."

"But she—"

"No argument, son. You know I'm right. She's a lady. You treat her with respect, no matter how mad you are."

Ben stared at Trace for a moment, then hung his head, the blond flap of hair hanging down his forehead. He kicked at the grass.

"OK, now my cattle can relax." Trace took a deep breath, wishing he could relax. With Beth only three feet away, his body was strung as tight as a bow.

"Ben, I'm sorry. I only signed you up because I thought you would like it," Beth said in a low voice.

The kid looked up, then crossed his arms. "I'm not going."

"But I can't get my money back, and the principal said the camp would be a lot of fun."

"Hey, the cattle, remember?" Trace pointed toward the Herefords grazing in the far pasture.

"She's sending me to camp! I hate her! My dad wouldn't make me go."

"Ben!" Beth crossed her arms and her eyes welled with tears. "I only did it—"

"Hey, everybody calm down!" Trace said in a demanding voice. With Beth so upset, his gut was in a hard knot. "What's wrong with camp? It might be fun. Any kid would want to go."

"It's stupid art camp. She never even told me. I'm not going. Only sissy, stupid geeks will be there."

"Fine!" Beth crossed her arms just like her son's. "I'll lose my deposit and you can sit here for a week in your *room.*" Without another word, she turned away from them and stomped across the field toward the house.

"Women!" Ben uncrossed his arms and shoved his hands in his pockets.

Trace couldn't help but laugh. How many times had he thought the same thing? Women, especially a woman a man thought highly of, could be frustrating.

"I think you hurt your mama's feelings," Trace said, remembering the look on Beth's face when she'd turned toward the house.

"I know, but I'm not going to no stupid art camp."

"Why not? You might have a good time." Trace took the hammer out of his belt and pounded a line of nails flush against the wood.

"You think?" Ben climbed the fence and jumped to Trace's side.

"Sure. Getting out of this one-horse town for a week sounds like a blast. Kids will probably swim every day. Eat hot dogs and ice cream. No parents to boss you around. Hey, you might even meet a girl."

"No way!"

Trace leaned forward and jokingly socked Ben in the shoulder. "Yeah, you might be missing out on a really good time. The way it stands now, you'll be sitting in your room for a week, sweating like a pig."

"Yeah, but—"

"Hey, I'm not here to change your mind. You do what you want."

Ben stared at Trace. "I'm still not going. All those art geeks? No way."

"Suit yourself." Trace shoved the hammer in his belt loop again. Ben was as stubborn as he'd been at that age. The kid needed to go to the camp, for Beth's sake. Hell, it sure wouldn't hurt him, and he might just learn something.

"Can I help you with the fences?" Ben asked as he climbed the fence again.

"Finished. But I'm heading to Abilene for a couple of hours to check on some paperwork. Want to go along?"

Ben balanced himself on the first wooden plank. "If I ask Mom, she won't let me. She's pretty cranky. She's always mad."

Trace dusted off his hands. He knew he

shouldn't, but he wanted to check on Beth to make sure she was OK. When she'd stomped off, she looked pretty upset. Besides, Ben and Beth needed a little space to cool off.

"Tell you what. I'll go up and ask her. Then if it's OK, we'll leave."

Beth heard the soft knock on the screen door. She dabbed her eyes with the tissue, then stuffed it in her pocket.

Trace.

She stood perfectly still near the sink and prayed he'd go away. After the other night, she'd promised herself she wouldn't come within ten feet of Trace Barlow. The way she was feeling right now, she didn't want to see anybody. If Ben hadn't run for the barn in such a fit, she would have been able to keep her promise for one more day.

What in the world was she going to do with her son?

Her chest ached and she drew in a deep breath.

"Beth." The now-familiar voice startled her. He knocked on the doorframe again. "Beth, I'd like to talk to you." Determination laced his tone, and she knew he wasn't going to go away.

She headed for the living room and found him framed in the screen door. He'd taken off his hat and rested it on the railing. In the shade of the porch, Trace Barlow appeared cool and concerned.

He smiled and she shivered. She swallowed and reminded herself of her promise. "Oh, God."

"What?"

"Nothing. I'm still so mad I'm talking to myself," she lied.

"Yeah, I can understand that. Can I come in? I'd like to ask you something."

She shook her head. "I'd rather be alone." But then she made the mistake of looking at him. His face was a study in anxiety, and she couldn't turn him away. "OK, come in."

Trace stepped into the living room, but stopped near the door. "I talked to Ben a little bit. Thought maybe you'd let him ride with me to Abilene this afternoon. I'll be back in a couple hours."

She shook her head. "After the way he acted, he needs to stay in his room."

"If he comes back to the house, you two are going to fight."

He was right. Beth clasped her hands together and wrung them. "I don't know what to do with him. Every move I make seems to be the wrong one."

"Hey." Trace took a step forward, then stopped. He dropped his gaze to the carpet; then suddenly his eyes were on her again. "You're doing a good job. He's going through one hell of an awkward stage, that's all. Ben's trying to stretch his wings." The empathy in his dark eyes had grown, and her muscles loosened a little.

"If I just knew for sure I'm making the right decisions. I thought he'd love the art camp."

"You've got to have more faith in yourself. He's a rebellious kid growing up without a dad. I've been there. It's not you, it's him."

She closed her eyes as her feelings overwhelmed her.

"You should be proud of what you've done. Besides, I survived growing up, and I'm a pretty good guy."

Beth opened her eyes and laughed lightly. Trace was a *very* good guy. "I know it's hard for Ben, too."

Trace closed the space between them and touched her shoulder for just a quick moment, yet it filled her with strength.

"So you don't think I'm going to ruin Ben?"

"No way."

Her entire body ached for his caring touch, for Trace Barlow to hold her and tell her everything was going to be OK, yet Beth fought it. She needed to be strong for Ben and for herself. Moving closer to Trace could only bring her a basketful of trouble.

"Thanks. I feel better," she managed.

"Is it OK if he goes to Abilene? I'll have him back before bedtime."

Bedtime, when she climbed into her double bed alone and her thoughts were consumed with

Trace. She dreamed about his arms around her, his lips on hers, his fingers touching . . .

God!

She needed to think of Ben and what was best for him. Her heart raced.

"I don't care! You seem to be better with him than I am," she snapped.

Trace stood there, hurt growing in his eyes. Then suddenly it turned to concern.

She was losing it. "Yes, he can go." She pressed her lips together and walked out of the room.

Trace pushed open the bank door, and he and Ben walked into the building. He had to deliver some papers to the manager and then they could head home. The kid had been sullen on the drive to Abilene.

That had been fine with Trace. All he could think about was Beth. Trace gritted his teeth. The woman had gotten under his skin. He'd known it for days now, but today had been the ultimate proof of how much she'd stolen his sanity.

When he'd seen the look on her face while she was trying to reason with Ben, his chest had tightened like he'd been roped. All he'd wanted to do was help her.

He'd never felt that way about any woman, not even his ex. Now all he was thinking about was protecting Beth from any more pain. That had been the real reason he'd offered to take Ben with him.

"Wow! Look at those," Ben said as they walked farther down the hall.

Trace had forgotten about the western artwork lining the walls of the Texas National Bank. He smiled. This would keep Ben busy while he did his paperwork.

"Wow, look at those!" They walked to the first painting, a herd of wild horses running along a ridge. Ben stared at the colorful image as if he'd never seen anything like it. "Look at the way the artist painted their manes. It looks like they're flying through the air."

Trace put his hand on Ben's shoulder. "I'm gonna do my banking. I'll be back in a while. You take your time and look at all the paintings."

"Yeah, Trace, whatever. I'll be here." Ben didn't take his eyes off the horses.

Fifteen minutes later Trace found Ben, still spellbound, in front of two paintings down the hallway. "What do you think?"

"This guy is awesome."

Trace pulled out the paper he'd stuffed in his pocket a few minutes ago. "Ben, take a look at this. There's a bunch of them at the teller's window."

The kid turned and grinned at Trace. "These paintings are way cool. Some of them are in that book you gave me."

"Yeah." Trace gazed at the one they were standing in front of. He didn't know anything about artistic talent, but he liked the painting. It showed Texas—horses and livestock and rodeos—in the right light.

His attention shifted back to Ben and the entry form he still held in his hand. "Says here they're having a western art contest for the Fort Worth Rodeo and Stock Show. You could enter something of yours."

Ben's eyes brightened. "A contest of western art?"

Trace held the entry form so he could see it. "You win five hundred dollars if you take first place, and your work will be put on display. They'll make a poster out of your entry and show it all across the country."

Ben stared at the entry form. "The country? And five hundred dollars. I could buy Mom something more than cool after I get those Nikes I've been wanting."

"True. And you could tell all the kids at camp you entered the contest."

Ben stared at the entry form and then at the painting behind them. "Camp? I told Mom I wasn't going."

Trace chuckled and patted Ben's shoulder. "She'll understand if you change your mind. Women do that a lot, too—change their minds, that is."

Ben tilted his chin and studied the ceiling for a moment. "Yeah, Mom's always changing her mind. Sometimes I think she's gonna get mad at me and she doesn't. Then when I'm sure she won't get mad at me, she does."

Trace laughed out loud. He was having trouble understanding Beth, too. The way Beth kissed told him she wanted him, but the next moment she was pushing him away.

But maybe he could help her now with Ben. The kid was really interested in entering the contest, and that just might get him to camp. Then Beth would be happy.

"Your mom's a good lady. Remember, it's the little things that'll make your mama happy. Most people are like that."

Yet Trace didn't believe for one minute Beth Morris was like any other person he'd ever met.

"She's confusing. She'll be yelling, then all of a sudden, she's bawling her eyes out." Ben shook his head. "I'm never gonna get a girlfriend."

Trace laughed hard. "You'll change your mind. Remember, your mama loves you. Do the little things she wants, and she'll be OK. So will you. It's pretty much your job to make her happy . . . you know, being the man in the family and all."

Ben jutted out his chin and squared his shoulders. "Yeah, I know that's my job." He looked down at the entry form and studied it for a moment. "Maybe I will enter. Do you think it'd make her happy if I went to her stupid art camp?"

"Yep. Maybe you could throw in that you're sorry you talked mean to her. That would surprise the heck out of her. You might even get one of her pretty smiles."

The memory of Beth's smile rose into his mind and Trace sucked in more air. Nothing could compare to that woman's pretty face when she was happy.

"Camp might not be so bad. Plus the five hundred dollars won't hurt me, either."

Trace patted Ben on the shoulder. "You're pretty sure you're gonna win, huh?"

Ben's lips broke into a grin. "Yeah, I'll win. You just wait and see."

TWELVE

Beth sat on the edge of Ben's bed next to her son. She couldn't help but smile. He had come home from Abilene happy and excited.

"Do you think I can win?" Ben glanced at the art contest entry form on his nightstand.

She reached out and touched Ben's shoulder. Every day he seemed to grow a little more. Soon he wasn't going to be her little boy anymore. Times like these, she cherished being a parent— times when it was rewarding and easy, when she knew she was doing a good job.

"I think you have as much chance as anyone. You need to remember it's not all about winning. Of course, that's fun, too. The best thing is that you're trying, participating in something you really like."

"Yeah, sure, Mom. But I want to win. I could use the money. And just think, my painting turned into a poster and sent across the United States!"

Beth laughed. "What are you going to enter?"

"It's gotta be something new. Trace and I saw

some western paintings at the bank, like the ones you and I looked at when we visited the museum. They were awesome. I want to do something like that."

"That's wonderful. But winning isn't everything. You might not."

"I know, but I've got to try. Trace told me on the way back he'd help me get the entry ready to mail." Ben's grin grew even wider. "That's the hard part. It has to be just right. Just the way the entry says."

Trace.

Just the mention of his name could make her heart start beating in a different way and her entire body quiver.

"Trace said when I get back from camp, he'll help me."

"So you're going to camp now?" Beth pressed her lips together in an effort to suppress her excitement.

"He said I need to go, and I guess he's right. I can finish my entry before I leave. I've already got an idea. If I win, the painting will be made into a poster. A poster for every rodeo in the country. Did I tell you that?"

Beth laughed and hugged Ben. "Yes, about one hundred times. I think it's wonderful."

Trace certainly knew how to talk Ben into what was good for him.

"Mom?" Ben sat up a little.

"Yes, honey?"

"You feeling all right? You've got that *gonna barf* look on your face again."

Beth laughed, tugged at the corner of Ben's blanket, and tucked it in a little. "I was just thinking about how happy you're going to be at camp, that's all. And when you're happy, I'm happy."

Ben nodded. "Yeah. Trace said it's the little things that make you happy."

Again she laughed. Trace was giving her son advice about moms—that was interesting. Her heart pounded harder against her ribs. She needed to stop thinking about the man, but that was impossible.

Beth stood and took a deep breath. It was going to be another long, lonely night.

"Uh, Mom?"

"Yes, Ben?" Goodness, she hoped she didn't have that look on her face again.

"I'm sorry . . . about today." Her son's voice cracked in the middle of his apology.

Beth looked at him. His expression was so serious she knew he meant the words he was saying. "I'm sorry I yelled at you, honey."

"Trace said I should make sure you know I don't hate you. I was just mad, that's all."

Beth leaned down and wrapped her arms around Ben. "It's OK. Families fight and then they make up. That's the nice thing about relatives. They'll always love you."

Half an hour later, after checking on Ben to make sure he was asleep, Beth found herself out on the porch. She was hoping the fresh air would make her sleepy.

A yellowy, square patch of light from Trace's window ran down the side of the barn and melted halfway across the pasture. Sultry night air, full of the promise of a long summer, danced around her. Beth filled her lungs and thought about everything that had happened today.

Trace had made such a difference in her and Ben's lives, and she'd snapped at him this afternoon.

Beth shuddered as she remembered the look in his eyes.

Carol Kelly had been right about the mentoring situation. Trace was a good influence on Ben, and she'd acted like she wasn't grateful. Even if he claimed to know nothing about kids or families, the man had changed their lives.

Beth brushed back the hair that was tickling her cheek. This afternoon he'd made it possible for Ben to be happy and excited about art camp. And now her son was enthusiastic about the contest, too.

She owed him a *big* apology.

Beth swallowed and shook her head. He must think she thought he'd overstepped his bounds—intruded. But she'd only acted that way because she was hurt and mad.

Had she really let him know how much his mentoring had helped Ben? Between fighting her attraction for him and being angry with Ben, she wasn't sure she had.

He was spending his valuable time with Ben even though he didn't have to, and she needed to say she was sorry.

Without thinking about anything else, Beth headed for the kitchen. The chocolate cake she'd baked while Trace and Ben had driven to Abilene was sitting on the counter.

She cut two huge pieces, placed them on a plate, and covered them in clear wrap. She'd walk down to the barn, hand the cake to Trace, say she was sorry, and come back to the house.

That was the least Trace Barlow deserved.

"Trace."

He heard her voice and at first thought he'd fallen asleep and was dreaming. The light tap on his closed door told him he wasn't.

"Trace, it's me."

His heart slammed up into his throat. He stood, crossed the room, and opened the door.

Beth stood outside, looking shy and vulnerable, her hair pulled back in its usual way, her blue eyes sparkling with anticipation. The soft blue T-shirt she wore was tucked into loose shorts, and tennis shoes covered her feet.

"Hey," was all he could manage as a deep happiness at just seeing her rolled through his body.

"Hi. I hope I'm not bothering you." She dipped her chin a little and Trace glanced down at his shoeless feet. After he'd dropped Ben off,

he'd changed into shorts and a T-shirt and tried
to take a nap, but with no success.

"No, not at all." He stepped back a little.
"Come on in."

Beth walked into his room and glanced
around. She nibbled on her bottom lip and nervously cleared her throat.

His breath caught in his throat at the sight of
her in his room.

Everything the woman did fascinated him.

Instantly, she looked at him. "Are you comfortable?"

He swallowed hard and wondered if she'd read
his mind. "Comfortable? Now?" The question
sent his body into overdrive.

She nodded toward the bed. "With living
here—the room and bath. Is it OK? Do you need
anything?"

"It's fine. Great. I've stayed in worse places,
believe me." He swallowed again and allowed
himself the luxury of just looking at her.

Yeah, he'd stayed in some dumps, but never
with such a great landlady.

"Good. I'm glad you're happy. I've . . . well,
I've never been a landlord before." She turned
and inspected the place again. "And the cattle?"

"They love your grass. Everything is perfect,
Beth. I have no complaints. Did you think I
did?" He couldn't help but stare at her. She
looked like an angel standing there staring back
at him.

He was happy she'd come to visit him. How

could he not be glad she was concerned if he was comfortable above her barn? Yet with Beth so close, he couldn't stop remembering the other night, when they'd wound up in each other's arms.

Trace reminded himself he had to quit thinking this way or there was going to be big trouble. "Can I help you with something? Is there a problem with Ben or anything else?"

Her eyes widened a bit, and suddenly she glanced down at what she was holding. "Oh! I came to apologize for snapping at you this afternoon. I brought you a peace offering."

"Hey, forget about this afternoon. I have."

She held out the plate. "Two pieces of a chocolate cake I baked after you left for Abilene. I thought you might like something sweet."

Yeah, but it wasn't cake he had an appetite for. Beth was the sweetest lady he'd ever met.

Trace took the plate from her and their fingers brushed for a quick moment. Her skin was cool against his fiery body.

"Yeah, I love sweet things."

Beth's gaze shot to his, her brow arching for a moment. The corners of her mouth tipped up a little. "Yes, I just bet you do."

He couldn't help but laugh. "I'd never expect a line like that from you."

"Well, doesn't everybody like candy, chocolate?"

"Right." He couldn't take his eyes off her. The

woman looked even more beautiful when she was flustered. God, he was crazy about her.

"I also brought you the cake to say thank you for talking to Ben today." Her voice was soft and held a whole lot of promises.

"I haven't done—"

"Don't be so modest. Yes, you have. It's about time you acknowledge what you've accomplished. Ben told me tonight he'll go to art camp, and he's so excited about the contest."

She shook her head a little and her ponytail bobbed up and down. "It's just wonderful. He even apologized for saying what he did this afternoon. You know how rare it is for a ten-year-old boy to say he's sorry?"

"About as rare as a twenty-something year old." Trace felt himself nod. Maybe he was better with kids than he'd thought.

But most of all, he wanted to help Beth. He loved seeing her happy and smiling, relaxed like this. His gaze drifted to her lips.

"When you asked to move out here, you said you'd help Ben. You've done a great job with him." Beth took a deep breath and her breasts stretched the soft T-shirt.

He could see the outline of her nipples against the material and blood hammered to his groin. God, he was sure Beth didn't even know how attractive she was.

His fingers tingled with the need to touch her. Trace wanted to hear her sigh again, feel her melt in his arms.

"Trace, don't you think so?"

Her question brought him out of his day-dream. "Think what?"

"That what has helped Ben most of all is having you around, knowing you'll be here to talk to when he needs a male opinion? He doesn't realize it, but I know he looks forward to seeing you."

Trace nodded, but mentoring a kid for a few hours a day was easy. He didn't want to make this something it wasn't. He'd never stuck to anything. He hadn't done it when he was married, and he knew he couldn't change. Only the rodeo was important to him.

Besides, helping a kid who wasn't his own was easy. He had no long-term investment.

"Beth, I don't know. This mentoring thing just happened because I was driving too fast. And I think helping Ben is just luck."

"It's more than that. Ben really likes you."

"I like the kid, too, but it doesn't make me an expert. I've always been a tumbleweed. I've never been devoted to anybody. That's pretty much how my life is."

"Why do you think that?"

He looked at her hard. "Hey, when my marriage started getting rocky, I didn't care. I split when times got tough. So did my old man and my mom. It's the way my family is. How could I be any different?"

* * *

Beth heard his words, but Trace's eyes said more. The worry in his gaze told most of his story. He believed what he was saying, and she couldn't let him, not after he'd affected their lives so completely. Trace was a good man.

She stepped forward and seized his hand.

His skin was as warm as she remembered it from the other night. Beth rubbed his fingers, and his calluses reminded her of all the work he'd done around Oak Creek.

She had to make him see he was different than he thought.

"Trace, look at how much you've helped Ben, and all the work you've done here at the ranch. A lot of men wouldn't have done half of what you have. Besides, I couldn't have stayed here if it wasn't for you and your cattle."

She squeezed his fingers again and gazed into his dark eyes, trying to make her point.

"Hell, I didn't do all that much. Besides, you helped me, too. If you hadn't let me come out to Oak Creek, I'd be in a big mess. Looks like I owe you. As far as the fences, I enjoyed cleaning up the place. And Ben—I like the kid. Don't make me out to be something I'm not, Beth."

He slipped his hand out of hers.

Beth's heart sank. She would not let him brush off what he'd done for Ben—for her. Maybe if they just talked for a little while, she could make him see.

Her eyes scanned his room. She'd expected it to be filled with rodeo trophies, plaques, and framed certificates, but there weren't any. She was surprised there was no evidence of his rodeo career.

"Would you like to sit down?" Trace stepped to the bed and smoothed the blanket.

"No, I'm fine. Really. Why don't you try the cake? There's a fork on the plate." Beth surveyed the dresser across the room. A simple picture frame sat in the middle next to his belt.

"Chocolate cake, my favorite. I didn't know you could bake cakes, too."

She turned back around and smiled. He was teasing her now. "I can do a lot of things you don't know about."

His face broke into a grin and he laughed. "Is that so?"

She felt herself grin as she crossed the room. The picture was probably of Trace at a rodeo. She picked it up. Someone had snapped a photo of a ranch house much like the one at Oak Creek, only smaller.

"Cake's great." Trace took another bite. "You make this from a box?"

She turned with the picture still in her hand. "Are you kidding? That's from scratch. I had a lot of time this afternoon, so I tried a new recipe." She ran her thumb around the frame of the picture. "Is this where you lived as a kid?"

Trace laughed and sat on his bed, the cake plate still in his hand. "Yeah, right. We mostly lived out of boxes in rented houses, one time a car. Never had a home like that when I was a kid. Never had much of anything."

Beth, carrying the picture, crossed the space between them and stood in front of him. He looked at her and smiled.

"That's the ranch I lost when I broke my leg, the property I'm trying to get back. Then you won't have to put up with me anymore." He laughed, and she knew he was kidding her again.

"Well, that'll be great. Maybe by then I'll have figured out how I can live without any cash."

"You'll find a way. Lots of cowboys looking to lease land. Most of them can pay more than I can. You'll be better off when I'm gone."

She studied the picture for a long time, then looked at Trace. He'd eaten one piece of cake, wrapped the other back up and placed the plate on the table next to his bed.

His dark, smoky eyes narrowed, and he arched a brow. He patted the space next to him. "You can sit down. I promise I won't bite."

She shook her head and smiled, knowing he'd reason out why she didn't want to sit on his bed.

Trace chuckled and inched his way to the corner of the bed. "There, you've got lots of space. You can sit over there." He pointed to the other side. "Lots of room."

She looked at the picture again. The ranch resembled Oak Creek a lot. Her mouth turned to dust. She knew deep down what Trace really wanted was a home.

Good Lord, she wanted to know more about

the man, yet she was afraid of what she'd find out. If she learned more about Trace she'd be more drawn to him—maybe even love him.

Her knees grew weak at the thought, and she sat on the corner of the bed, as far away from Trace as possible.

"Someday I'm gonna own that place free and clear." Trace pointed to the picture she still held in her hand.

"Oh." Her temples throbbed. He'd said the words so simply, yet underneath them, she could hear the sincerity in his voice.

She knew far too well what it was like to want a home, a place where a person could be safe. A place where one could have a family.

"Yeah. Someday no one will be able to take my ranch away from me."

Beth drew in a deep breath. Trace's aftershave whirled around her and made her dizzy. The warm, thick feeling she'd been fighting took control of her body and she gave up fighting it. All she wanted to do was lean closer and touch him, encourage him. But it wasn't safe.

She forced herself to look around the room again.

Not one thing about any rodeo. When Ray was alive, the walls of their apartment had been covered with ribbons and pictures.

"I'm surprised you don't have a hundred and one trophies filling up this place," she said.

Trace took the picture out of her hands, stared at it for a long moment, and then placed it next to the cake. "Yeah, I used to do that. Every place I moved, I'd put my ribbons out, my trophies. Then I earned enough money to buy my ranch."

His voice was low, and he glanced at the picture. "When I moved in—well, hell, I just left the stuff in the boxes."

Ray had been so different. The more awards he'd won, the more he'd wanted. Trace seemed unusual in that way. She'd never met a cowboy like Trace Barlow, and her heart nearly stopped at the thought.

"You'll get your place back, I'm sure." It made her feel good that Trace wanted a home— needed a home.

"Thanks. I hope so." He shifted and, in doing so, moved a little closer. Trace turned and really looked at her, his eyes growing shadowy again.

She studied his face. Trace's eyes held a huge amount of kindness. He wasn't as handsome as Ray had been, yet Trace was just as attractive.

Beth let her gaze slide farther. His lips were thin. Usually they formed a grim line. But now Trace's lips curved up at the corners and she could tell he was about to smile.

"Go on," she said.

"Go on, what?" He shifted more.

"You look like you're about to smile. Go ahead."

He laughed and his lips lifted at the corners. A bit of chocolate frosting was hiding in the right corner of his mouth. Without thinking, she reached out and touched his face with her index finger. "I swear you're as bad as Ben when—"

He lifted his chin a little and his eyes closed. Before she could pull her hand away, he touched her finger with his tongue. It was warm and wet. Without any hesitation, Beth leaned close and wrapped her arms around Trace.

Her lips found his and she opened for him. Trace's tongue plunged into her mouth and he moaned. Beth combed her fingers through his thick hair and pulled him closer to her.

He tasted like a whole box of chocolates, and she wanted to kiss him forever.

Trace wasn't surprised when Beth leaned over and kissed him on the lips.

Hell, he was getting used to that look of hers, the one that told him she was falling into this situation as deeply as he was.

Beth moaned her own special, sexy way, and for a moment, Trace thought he just might go crazy. Then he kissed her harder.

God, how he wanted this woman in his bed, naked and next to him.

He let his hands and lips roam over her, touching her here, licking her there. To him, Beth's face and body were perfect, and he wanted to read each part of her like a blind man—with his eyes closed.

She ran her hand up his thigh to his manhood, and he groaned, enjoying the strong sensations she created as blood pooled in his groin and throbbed.

But just as suddenly as she'd fallen into his arms, she was gone, standing on the other side of the room, her chest heaving, her arms crossed.

He gasped for air and then drank in as much as he could. Having Beth ripped out of his embrace was like being bucked right off of a bull and hitting the ground hard—like the sense had been knocked out of him.

Yet even in his agitation and confusion, he knew their kissing could lead to only one thing, and making love would put them in a pot of trouble. Beth needed a man who would stick, not a tumbleweed like himself. Besides, Trace didn't want to carry around memories of Beth for the rest of his life.

"I should *not* have let that happen."

Her sweet voice acted like a fan to the blaze still growing inside him. Trace stood and took a step toward her. More exasperation and bewilderment rushed into her eyes.

He wanted to make love to Beth in the worst way, and he could tell by the way she looked at him she did, too.

"Trace, we have to think about this."

"I'm finished thinking." He took another step toward her.

"I've got to get back to the house." She crossed the room and opened the door. Her face was still flushed from his whiskers and their kisses.

Before he could say another word, she was gone. His groin pounded with need for Beth.

But Trace knew it was better. He and Beth weren't right for each other. The only thing he needed to do was win the Abilene roping competition and get out of Beth's life forever.

THIRTEEN

"Ben, honey, can't you bring your work up to the house?" Beth stopped in the middle of the field and stared at her son. He had that determined look on his face, and she knew she wasn't going to be able to talk him out of dragging her down to the barn.

Beth's breath caught in her chest. She hadn't forgotten what had happened down at the barn two nights ago.

She'd made such a fool of herself!

Her face tingled hot at the thought. She drew her bottom lip into her mouth and nibbled on it. Thank goodness, in the last forty-eight hours she'd managed to stay as far away from Trace as was humanly possible.

"What's the matter, Mom? You've got that look on your face again. Are you getting sick?"

Ben's question brought her back to the middle of the dusty field where she was standing. "I'm fine. I have a lot to do at the house. I certainly don't have time to come down to the barn, Ben."

Ben's face fell, and Beth felt like she'd been

kicked in the stomach. What was wrong with her? Ben wanted to show her his work, and she was acting like a silly, shy teenager. If Trace came into the barn while they were there, she'd just say hello and that would be the end of it.

Her pounding heart told her that might not be what would happen, but then she looked at Ben. He was staring at her, waiting. How could she disappoint him because of her out-of-control feelings?

"Don't you want to see what I've painted for the art contest?"

"Yes, of course, I do." She walked to him and mussed his hair. "I want to see all your artwork. All the time."

He grabbed her hand and pulled her along. "Come on, then. I know you're gonna love it."

They ran across the field to the barn, and Ben opened the wooden door. Beth prayed she wouldn't see Trace.

Thank goodness, the main part of the barn was empty. She didn't dare look up at his room as her son pulled her down the hallway to his artwork.

Ben threw open the door. "What do you think? Is it good enough?" He ran in and stood by a large poster board. Ben had created a collage of rodeo images—horses, cowboys, and cowgirls—all drawn together with a rope. The primary colors called out to anyone who looked at the drawing.

Beth gasped with joy. "Oh, Ben, it's wonderful."

"I think it's great, too."

The familiar deep voice startled her. Trace was standing behind her.

With him so close, all she could think about was the way he'd kissed her the other night, how good his hands had felt on her body, and how she'd wanted him to strip her clothes away and touch her—make love to her.

Good Lord! She was losing her mind.

"Trace! How ya doing?" Ben sang out. His face turned into one big smile.

Beth, her body humming, forced herself to look at Trace. She didn't want Ben to suspect anything was wrong between them. "Hi, Trace. How are you?"

He nodded, his eyes narrowing as he looked at her. "I'm OK."

She drew in a breath and tried to steady herself, but her efforts to feel normal weren't working.

"You getting ready for Abilene?" Ben asked.

"Yep, takes place right after you come home from camp."

Beth's body grew more tense.

With her growing attraction for Trace, she'd forgotten about the rodeo and how much it was a part of his life—how if he won at Abilene he'd be gone, out of their lives forever. Or maybe he wouldn't come back if there was an accident.

"I'd better get back to the house. I'm baking cookies for Ben to take to camp. He leaves tomorrow." Her head was pounding as she crossed to the door.

"But, Mom, I want—"

"Ben, I have to get back to the house." She should be able to handle this situation better, but she couldn't. With Trace so close, her nerves were absolutely raw, and she needed to put some distance between them. She turned and hurried out of the barn.

Halfway across the field, Beth stopped. She was out of breath and her chest was aching. She turned and looked back. Trace's window faced their house. Just a few short days ago she'd been up in his room, ready to make love to the man.

Her nerves sprang to life and the need for him made her feel faint. She'd wouldn't be able to quiet her desires soon.

Yet she needed to forget about Trace. She had a son to raise and a home to provide for him. There was no way she could let herself get involved with Trace. More than ever, today proved she had to stay away from him.

The man stole any rational thoughts she had.

Soon Trace would be out of their lives. Ben didn't need to experience losing someone, either.

Beth took another deep breath and continued to stare at the barn. Trace was going to Abilene soon. After that, there would be more rodeos, more danger. She couldn't face loving and losing him.

* * *

"I'm not going to enter."

Trace glanced at Ben, who stood in the middle of the room staring at his poster. For the last few seconds, he'd forgotten about the kid. He'd been too busy staring at the open door Beth had raced out of.

Before she'd sprinted from the room, he'd seen the pained look in Beth's gaze and sensed right away she was uncomfortable with him around.

Why in the hell had he come down to Ben's room, anyway? He gritted his teeth. Because when he'd heard Beth's voice, wild horses couldn't have kept him away. He'd jogged down the stairs like a bull in heat when the heifers were let into the ring.

"Trace?"

The sound of his own name pulled him back. Ben was looking at him. "What did you say?"

"I said I'm not entering the poster in the contest." Ben crossed his arms and glared at the open door.

"Why not?"

" 'Cause Mom acted like she didn't like it."

"Did she say so?" Trace couldn't believe Beth didn't like Ben's work for the contest. He wasn't a critic, but he knew the poster was right up there with any winner.

"No! She said it was wonderful, but did you see the way she ran out of here? She's usually hugging and kissing me when I show her what

I've been working on. She hates it. I'm not going to enter it now."

The blood pounded to his temples and Trace shook his head.

Now I've done it.

If he hadn't come down to see Beth, she could have talked to Ben more and the kid would feel better about his work.

This goat rope was just one more reason he needed to keep away from Beth—stay out of her life so she could raise her son properly—and it proved even more he wasn't any good at this family stuff.

"Your mother wanted to get back to the house to bake you some cookies. Doesn't mean she didn't like your poster."

Ben's mouth drew into a firm line. "I could tell she didn't like it. It's no good and I'm not gonna enter it. Didn't you see the look on her face?"

Yeah, he'd seen her eyes, too. They'd held the same expression they had the other night. The minute he and Beth were within twenty feet of each other, a fire started to blaze in both of them.

But he wasn't about to make her uncomfortable. And when she'd raced out of the barn, it was evident she wasn't happy.

"I should tear up this piece of junk," Ben said.

"The poster is good." Trace nodded at the entry. "It's a winner."

Ben recrossed his arms. "No, it isn't. And now

I have to go to that stupid art camp. I can't draw. Mom's driving me crazy. The last couple days she's been grumpy! Women! I'll see you next week, Trace." The kid stomped across the room and out the door.

Trace stared at the poster. Ben was wrong. The poster was an example of some of his best work. The blue entry form was on the table next to the wall.

Trace crossed the room and picked it up. At least there was one problem he could remedy.

Beth sat on the couch and stared at the opposite wall. Her son had been gone for almost two days, and she still wasn't used to how incredibly quiet and lonely the house was.

She stood, crossed the room to the end table, and clicked on the low light. Then she swallowed over the lump in her throat. She'd expected her son to write her one of the postcards she'd tucked between his socks and underwear, but none had come.

The day Ben left, he'd acted so crabby. When she'd asked him about the art contest, he'd completely ignored her, then told her he wasn't entering, no matter what she said.

Shaking her head, she headed for the porch. At least outside the air was cool. Although the days were turning hot with summer, the nights still offered relief.

The screen slammed behind her, and Beth

found her usual porch chair. Would she ever understand Ben? Would they be able to spend a few hours together without arguing? She pressed her lips together and drew in a deep breath.

The lump in her throat grew and tears threatened. Beth swiped at her eyes and straightened her shoulders. There was no way she was going to be a crybaby about her dilemma with Ben. She needed strength for her son's sake.

They'd been through tough times before, and they'd make it through these, too. Beth studied her fingernails. Maybe she was being too optimistic. She had some long hard years in front of her with Ben.

Beth glanced up when she heard footsteps. Trace was making his way up the path toward the house.

Her heart began pounding erratically.

At least they'd been able to avoid each other for the past few days. She'd even managed not to think of him her every waking hour.

Beth laughed softly. No, she thought of him every ten minutes when she was awake and dreamed about him all night long.

She stood, ready to run into the house. Then she thought better of it. She'd look silly scampering away from him.

If it was the last thing she did, she had to get over her attraction to Trace. But she wasn't sure how to do that.

He came closer to the porch. Even in the faint light, his white T-shirt accented his tan and his dark hair, and his dark blue shorts showed off his strong legs.

Goodness, he was a sight!

Beth took a deep breath and held it, hoping her muscles would relax. She had to stop reacting this way. She stood and stepped back.

"Hey," was all he said as he stopped at the bottom of the steps.

"Hi." Beth's heart crashed against her ribs. Her skin was actually tingling.

He held up the cake plate and smiled. "Wanted to get this back to you."

Beth stared at the plate, afraid to let her gaze drift to his face. Had it been only a few nights ago when she'd kissed him until her entire body ached and begged to be touched?

"You doing OK?" He hitched his foot on the first step as he always did.

"I'm fine. Never been better." She sliced the edge of her hand through the air to let him know she was great.

"I just thought with Ben gone, you might be feeling . . ." Trace cleared his throat and scraped his toe against the first step.

Beth heard the concern in his voice. As usual, it melted her heart a little. He really was a friend. It wasn't his fault she couldn't keep her hands and lips off him.

"Just wanted to bring this back." He held out the plate again. "Thanks again for the cake. I enjoyed it."

Beth felt her face heat. She was acting like she

was mad at him, and all he'd come over for was to return her plate. He must think her personality was split—the jump-your-bones Beth and the aloof one.

She was an adult and didn't have to behave like some lustful maniac when she was around him, did she? At the thought, she chuckled.

"Something I missed?" He raised his dark brows.

"No, I'm just a little cranky. Guess I miss Ben more than I thought I would. He really is a lot of company."

"I bet."

"Except I don't miss his complaining."

Trace shook his head. "That kid sure knows how to push your buttons."

She laughed again. Why did she always feel happy around this man? "You think so?"

"The other day when you ran out of the barn, he told me you didn't like his poster. I think that's the reason he didn't want to enter it."

So that was it.

She'd been so distracted trying to get Trace out from under her skin, she hadn't thought about Ben's feelings or his work. "I never seem to get the parenting thing right, do I?"

"You're being a little hard on yourself." His voice was filled with consideration, and it grabbed at her heart.

"Because of me he didn't enter the contest. And when he comes back from camp, it's going to be too late."

Trace dug in his pocket, pulled out a slip of paper, and handed it to her. Beth squinted but couldn't read the print in the dim light.

"It's a receipt from the post office. I entered Ben's work. He might get mad, but that's tough. His painting was too good not to be part of the contest."

Trace smiled like a kid, his lips pulling into his all-too-familiar devastating grin. Beth closed her eyes for a moment. She'd never, ever known a man like Trace.

When she opened her eyes, he was still staring at her, drinking her in like a fine wine. Beth's heart beat into her throat. She shook her head and reminded herself Trace was just being nice.

"Thanks, Trace. I never thought of entering it for him." Because of the lump in her throat, she couldn't bring her voice higher than a whisper.

"Hey, are you OK?" He climbed the stairs and stood beside her.

His warmth and familiar scent surrounded her. A whirlwind of confusion swept over her.

"I'm fine, really. Just missing Ben and feeling bad about not paying attention to his poster." She crossed her arms and hugged herself.

"The kid probably won't even remember." Trace wrapped his arm around her shoulders.

Beth's knees turned to jelly.

"I shouldn't have come down from my room when I did the other day. You two didn't have a chance to talk about his entry."

She laughed nervously. Her skin was tingling

with just the small amount of contact. She stepped back, away from his touch. "Don't be silly. Ben and I usually end up yelling at each other."

His brows knitted together, accenting the confusion in his eyes.

She was acting silly again. He'd just put his arm around her to comfort her and she was behaving as if he were making a pass.

Good Lord, she was no good around men, no matter what their age. Well, he'd been far too considerate for her to hurt his feelings. She had to make up for it.

She waved the post office receipt at him. "Let me go get my purse and I'll reimburse you for the postage and the entry fee."

Trace put his hand up like a stop sign. "No way. I wanted to help Ben. Forget about it."

"Trace." She crossed the porch. "At least let me give you another piece of cake. Then maybe when you're in a sugar stupor, I can poke some money in your pocket."

"Chocolate again?"

She nodded and felt herself smile. What was that saying about a way to a man's stomach? Or was it his heart? "Yes, I made another chocolate cake. And not from a box, either."

He laughed. "I was only teasing you the other night."

When she'd kissed him until her toes curled. Obviously he hadn't forgotten what had happened, either.

"I'd love a piece of cake."

He'd been so nice to Ben, so concerned. "I've got milk that's as cold as a hundred-foot well."

Trace licked his lips. Then he smiled again and butterflies took flight in her stomach.

She shoved them away. What was wrong with her? The man just wanted dessert. She had to get control of herself. Beth really looked at Trace and tried to smile despite the way her heart was beating.

He smiled back and raised a brow. "Mighty nice of you to offer me dessert."

Beth nodded and headed for the front door. A piece of cake and a glass of milk was all the man was going to get from her.

FOURTEEN

Trace watched Beth move around the kitchen. A moment ago, she'd told him to make himself comfortable, and he'd sat in the wooden chair at the small table.

But he wasn't all that relaxed. Watching Beth, who looked so at home in the small kitchen in her T-shirt and shorts, and feeling calm was a tough combination to handle.

When she turned from the counter and walked toward him, he swallowed hard.

Each time he looked at Beth, she seemed more beautiful than the time before. Tonight she wore her hair loose, and it framed her face prettily. But the attraction wasn't about pretty blue eyes or the way her lips tilted up when she was happy, not at all.

Beth was almost perfect—everything good. She was strong, someone who knew how to fight for what she believed in, and she could laugh about her problems, too. Beth possessed everything he'd always wanted in a woman but never figured he could have.

"I cut you a big piece of cake," she said, standing at the table. Just being with her made him feel there wasn't anything in the world he couldn't do.

She placed the plate on the table, then added a paper napkin and fork on the side. "There you go."

"Great," he forced himself to say and looked up at her again.

"I'll get you some milk."

Beth walked to the other side of the kitchen and Trace couldn't take his eyes off her. Her hips, just the right size, swung easily, and the motion moved fluidly down her thighs to her well-proportioned calves.

She looked like an angel and cooked like one, too. Trace clenched his jaw and reminded himself he needed to quit thinking about Beth this way. It was never going to work out between them. Besides, there were other women he could call when the need struck.

He stared at her as she poured a large glass of milk. After knowing Beth, Trace was sure he wouldn't want to be with another woman for a long time.

No one could make him this happy. He loved talking to her about Ben, the ranch, or their lives.

I like just being with her.

The thought tore at any calm he had left. His manhood throbbed and he gritted his teeth against it. He'd never felt this way about any other woman, yet he had to stop his foolish thinking.

He wasn't her type, and she wasn't his.

She was aching for commitment, and he wasn't capable of giving it.

"Here's your milk."

She'd placed a tall glass in front of him and now she was smiling again. Her eyes were sparkling.

Trace knew, without a doubt, Beth was the kind of woman who'd be a man's partner—help him, cheer him on. She'd expect the same.

"Thanks. Great," he managed to say.

She moved around the table, away from him. His body begged for her to be close again. Beth pulled out a chair and sat.

Trace lifted his fork, looked at Beth, and smiled. She was sitting prettily, her fingers laced in front of her.

"You aren't going to join me?"

She shook her head and her hair danced around her shoulders. "No. I had a huge piece after dinner. Go ahead. Enjoy."

Her voice was like a musical instrument, sweet and happy-sounding. He wanted to savor all of her—take her into his arms and kiss her sweet lips again, lead her to her bed and make love to her all night long.

He gritted his teeth. The only way to harness these feelings was to get the hell out of here, put some distance between himself and this woman who took every one of his sensible thoughts and threw them out the window.

"You know, I've got to get going." He started to push his chair back.

"But—" She reached across the table and touched the back of his hand for a quick moment.

He shifted his gaze to hers. She'd laced her hands again, her eyebrows knitting. "How silly, Trace. It's Saturday. You probably have better things to do than sit here and eat cake. I'll wrap it up and you can take your dessert with you. Do you have a date?"

It took a few seconds for her words to sink in. Then he laughed out loud, and Beth's expression turned to hurt.

"I'm not laughing at what you said. I just haven't had a date since high school, and then I don't think you'd call it that."

"Oh, I just thought . . . Well, you're single and all." The wrinkle between her brows lessened.

His gut eased a little bit.

"You don't date at all?" Surprise laced her voice.

"Nah. Dating means getting involved, and that's not what I want to do." He took a forkful of cake and ate it.

God, the woman could bake a cake.

"Well, I certainly understand not dating that much. Sometimes it can be real work."

He studied her for a moment, then rubbed his jaw with his thumb. "Yeah. Too much work,

when you're not comfortable with the person."
His words reminded him how content he always
felt with Beth.

She nodded. "I'd rather be in my own kitchen,
just enjoying myself."

Maybe Beth was enjoying herself, too. The
thought made Trace happy. "It's the simple
things that make me happy. Some women don't
understand that. Like sitting on a horse and
watching the sunset."

Beth smiled. "Right. Or going into Branding
and eating pizza."

Trace heard himself laugh. "Seeing Ben smile
when he shows off his artwork."

"Baking a cake."

Trace took another bite of the chocolate
dream and swallowed. "Eating chocolate cake."

"Or sitting out on the porch and—"

Beth stopped in the middle of her sentence
and looked at Trace. He knew immediately what
she was thinking about.

He told himself to forget about what had happened between them, yet his gut tensed again.
He shoved another piece of cake into his
mouth, chewed and swallowed. "This is one
good cake," he said, working hard to change
the subject.

She tilted her chin and laughed self-consciously.
"Thanks." Then she leveled her gaze and studied
him for a minute. "You should date, Trace. You
must get lonely."

Beth looked incredibly pretty when she was being direct, and he knew he wouldn't have any trouble staring at her forever.

"I learned a long time ago I'm not the type of man to deal with that sort of thing. It's best for everybody I stay footloose."

"But just dating—"

"I made a mess out of my marriage. I was always out with my rodeo buddies. I was too concerned with what I wanted and not what she needed. It was pretty much my fault."

He ate another forkful of cake. "Besides, like I said, with my family history, I'm not the type to get tied down."

Something more serious slipped into her eyes as she watched him.

"But you were young when you were married. We all make mistakes. Look what you've done with Ben and the ranch. And you helped me out, too."

He nodded. "I'm so used to being a loner. I couldn't change now. Besides, a lot of people get married young and make it work."

"True. I'm not sure Ray and I would have lasted, though." More trouble filled her blue eyes, and Beth combed through her hair with her delicate fingers.

He fought the urge to reach over and touch her—not in a sexual way, but just to comfort her a little. "I'm sure you'd make a great partner."

She laughed a little and blinked. "Ray didn't want to get married, but Ben was on the way. He had a rodeo career to worry about. I should have . . . but I let my feelings get away from me when we were dating. He always told me I should be happy he did the right thing."

"It takes two to tango."

"He had his own goals. We were both too young and we both gave up dreams. He was so busy with rodeos he didn't have time to be a husband or a father. I don't want to make the same mistake again. I can't. I have Ben to think about now." Her words were soft, not laced with anger or grief.

"Right. You won't let any cowboy in your life."

Trace's words hung in the air like a thick fog and Beth's eyes widened. God, she was everything he'd always wanted in life—a good woman who cared deeply, a woman who would fight for what she believed in.

But he wasn't a fool, either.

Beth deserved someone who could give her what she needed.

She kept staring at him with those darned soft blue eyes.

"I . . . just don't want to lose someone I . . ." She shifted her gaze from his and studied her hands for a moment. "Oh, we're getting so serious now." Beth looked at the chocolate crumbs on his plate. "And chocolate has the reputation of making people happy."

* * *

Trace patted his flat stomach. "I'm happy. Finish what you were going to say."

Beth forced her gaze away from his and looked at her hands again. A moment ago she was about to be too honest—was about to tell him she couldn't take the chance of losing someone again. Thank goodness she'd stopped herself. She wasn't about to confide in Trace.

"Oh, I'm just talking. Really, it's nothing." She looked at him and their gazes connected. "You should go out. You were young when your marriage broke up. You should give yourself another chance."

He laughed. "I told you before, don't make me out to be something I'm not. For the good of women all over Texas, I'm not going to get serious with anyone."

He leaned forward, his elbows on his thighs, and Beth let her gaze follow.

"Trace, that scar!" She couldn't stop herself from reaching out and touching the wide line dividing his knee in half. "I've never noticed it before. Is that from when you broke your leg?"

His warmth wound around her fingers and floated to her heart. She shifted her attention to his face.

His eyes had turned a darker brown. He cleared his throat and gazed down at her fingers, which still rested on his bare knee, then laughed cynically. "That's what happens when a bull goes one way and the rider goes underneath him. No big deal."

"It looks like a very big deal to me."

"Maybe. Just a battle scar. Should have given up bull riding long before this happened. But . . ." He stopped and sucked in a deep breath.

"But what?" She craved to know everything about him.

"I was pretty determined to pay off my ranch so no one could take it away from me. So I rode that bull when I should have stopped. A man should know his limits."

"Your ranch meant a lot to you. I understand." And she did too. "You and I are the same in that way. I never had a real home till Oak Creek." She stopped and studied her hands. What was she saying? She wasn't sure, but with her heart racing so, she didn't care.

"The same?"

"Wanting a home. In other ways, too. We both had marriages that didn't work."

Trace nodded but didn't say a word.

"And we both are determined not to get involved again." She scrutinized his face. Trace Barlow really did want a home, a place to feel as if he belonged. All his words about not making him to be something he wasn't were just words—maybe even a way of protecting himself.

"Beth, I think you know me too well." Trace whispered her name just the way she liked to hear it said.

She nodded. "Yes, maybe I do." A thousand butterflies rose in her chest.

"We're both thinking about the *same* thing now."

She nodded. God, she was falling in love with Trace and there wasn't anything she could do about it. And at the moment, she didn't care.

Without another word, he seized her wrist and brought it to his chest. He pressed the palm of her hand against his T-shirt.

His heart was beating as hard as hers, and Beth could see the need in his eyes.

"Trace."

He wrapped his fingers around her other wrist and gently pulled her up with him. They were only inches apart. His sweet breath feathered against her skin and she inhaled it.

She wanted so much to be a part of him.

As if he could read her mind, his arms wrapped around her, and he brought her close and kissed her lips. Beth was more than ready for his mouth on hers. She pressed close to him, fitting against his body perfectly.

They kissed as if they'd kissed a thousand times before, their tongues dancing with each other, their bodies moving to the rhythm of their need.

A few dizzy moments later, Trace cradled her easily in his arms, making her feel weightless. He leaned into her, his lips against her ear.

"Where?" was all he said, yet she knew exactly what he was asking.

She told herself this was crazy, that she was acting crazy, but she didn't care. For once she wanted to be crazy—insane with Trace Barlow.

"Down the hall to the right."

He carried her easily to her room and placed her on the bed. The summer moonlight shone through the cotton curtains and splashed the bed in a silvery glow.

Her heart pounded and her body ached for him.

He stood by the side of the bed and looked down at her. Even in the pale light, she could see his gaze narrow as he stared at her. He leaned down and ran his fingers through her hair, then touched her cheek.

The slight caress caused a deep throbbing below her waist. Beth caught his hand with her own and brought it to her lips. Her tongue drew a circle around the tip of his index finger.

Deep in her heart, she knew he was wrong for her, and she wasn't right for him. Trace needed someone who understood him, who took him as he was.

His fingers touched her face again and stroked all her worries away. For the first time in her life, she didn't care what was right or wrong.

"Beth," he whispered. He kissed and suckled her breast through her shirt.

She sighed, then moaned and arched toward him. She wouldn't let herself think about anything but making love to Trace.

A moment later, he stripped off his clothes,

then hers, and was beside her. Naked, they fit together even more perfectly than she'd imagined. He tightened his arms around her and kissed her with tenderness at first, then let his need guide his lips and hands.

Beth heard herself moan again.

She lifted with each touch, delighted in each move. Her hands roamed over him and deep currents of desire ran through her. A thick yearning took the place of any rational thoughts.

She gazed at Trace above her. The moonlight painted his face as he moved against her, his eyes closed, his mouth relaxed and sensual. He opened his eyes and touched his lips to hers.

"I've wanted you for so long," he whispered against her skin, his breath coming faster. "But I want what happens between us to be slow, good for you, too."

"I don't feel like going slow," she said huskily, thrusting her hips to his. Trace's manhood throbbed against her belly and a deep, sweet, lustful demand pulsated through her entire body.

"Slow and easy, long . . ." His fingers brushed her breast, circling her nipple. And then his hand drew a straight line from her breast to her belly and he stroked her gently.

Beth lifted to meet his touch, moaning softly, her eyes closed, her breath coming faster.

"Slow and easy," he whispered against her ear as his fingers rubbed and went farther, finding another place that was waiting for him. He stroked and petted until Beth could not wait any longer.

"Trace, I want you."

He looked into her eyes again, and his lips curved into a smile. "I want you, too, sweetheart—wanted you from the moment I saw you." Trace moved above her, between her legs, and found her. A moment later he pressed deep within her.

They rocked together, meeting each other's needs—touching, moaning, calling each other's name, finding feelings they didn't even know existed. Soon they found a rhythm no one else in the world possessed.

Beth felt Trace tense, his muscles growing rigid, his breath coming faster. She went with him to that far-off place where all she thought about was making love to Trace, being a part of the man she loved.

Suddenly she was saying his name over and over, wanting him deeper inside her. Her world burst into a thousand moonbeams with stars attached to each one.

"Come on, baby, come with me."

His words lifted her and spun her around, drew her into the moonlight and sunlight and starlight. In that painfully beautiful moment, Beth knew she'd never be the same.

His breath was fast and wove around her. Trace threw back his head and tensed for the last time. He collapsed against her, his lips next to her cheek.

"Beth . . . Beth, God, I love you."

"I love you, too."

Trace woke and reached for her. She lay next to him, her body curled against his as if they'd lain together every night for years. He stroked her arm and she stirred, sighing. In a matter of seconds, he was hard and throbbing against her.

"Hey," she said, not much above a whisper. She arched and pushed her back against his chest.

He leaned down a little, touching his lips to the top of her shoulder. He licked her sweet skin, his tongue drawing circles, tasting her. Her body was soft and creamy, and he knew he'd be happy if this moment went on forever.

"Trace." She turned her head slightly. "Kiss me."

He fingered her hair, bringing the soft strands to his lips and made a smooching sound.

She laughed gently, and music filled the air. "No, not my hair."

He laughed, too. He always felt like he was on top of the world when he was within fifty feet of Beth. He wrapped his arm around her waist and pulled her closer.

She giggled again.

"Kiss you where?" he asked, wanting to tease her, wanting to make her happy, wanting Beth to experience the same happiness he was feeling. He didn't wait for an answer. His lips touched her shoulder and strung kisses across her soft skin.

Beth shivered with delight.

"You like my kisses?" he asked, his voice deep with the throbbing need to be inside her again.

"I love your *everything*, Trace." She turned gently and faced him. "Kiss me again."

"And where would you like them this time, ma'am?"

Her hand stroked down his body, her fingers first catching in his chest hair. Then she drew an imaginary line to his throbbing manhood.

"Oh!" she said, yet her fingers didn't jerk away.

He groaned and reached for her, kissing the rise of her breasts, her nipples, sucking the tips. He painted kisses up her throat, across her lips and her cheeks.

After they'd made love one more time, Beth snuggled against him and sighed in her sleep as he stroked her arm gently, and Trace stared at the ceiling.

He knew he'd never forget Beth. Never in a million years could he forget her sighs or those sexy moans when she was ready to meet her own needs.

She loved him. A woman like Beth didn't fake anything in her life. When she'd told him she loved him, Trace knew she meant it.

And he was sure he loved her.

He'd never felt this way about a woman before, and probably never would again. But he knew, deep down, things didn't work out when he gave his heart. Their connection would break, but he wasn't going to let himself think about that now.

For now he was going to love Beth Morris with all that was in him.

FIFTEEN

"Why are you kissing *him*?"

Beth pulled out of Trace's arms and her hand flew to her chest. She pressed her palm against her racing heart and turned toward the voice.

Ben stood on the porch in his pj's, staring at them.

He'd been home from art camp for two days, and she and Trace had been meeting after Ben went to sleep.

Feeling like a wayward teenager, Beth's face flashed hot with embarrassment. "Ben, you scared the daylights out of me. What in the world are you doing up?"

"It's hot in my room. Why were you kissing *him*?" Ben's arms hung by his sides, his fingers curled into fists. His pajamas were wrinkled and his blond hair mussed and tangled.

He stared at his mother and Trace, his gaze a study of hurt and bewilderment. Beth felt stunned. Ben adored Trace. Why would he be so upset?

In confusion, Beth backed away from Trace.

There was no use lying to Ben. He was old enough to know what was going on, and not telling the truth would only make the situation worse.

Yet she never anticipated having her son find them here and having to explain.

"Ben, I . . ." She stopped. His hurt expression stole all her words.

Trace cleared his throat and took a step forward. "Your mother and I—"

"You shut up. You're nothing but a loser! I hate you! You aren't like my dad. My dad was a big rodeo star, a hero." Ben screamed at Trace and then glared at both of them. Suddenly the boy turned his anger on Beth. "You were kissing him. He's nothing like my dad! Is that why you sent me to camp? So you could get rid of me?"

Beth's bafflement increased. She never would have predicted this reaction from Ben. "Honey, I sent you to camp because I thought you would enjoy it." She drew in a deep breath and tried to calm herself. She had no idea how to handle this situation.

"I hate you and I hate him." Ben's blue eyes flashed hurt and anger. "He's not even a winner like my dad. I'm not going to listen to you anymore."

Ben turned and ran into the house.

"Beth, maybe—"

"I've got to go to him." Beth followed Ben, her heart racing. She found her son in his room, sitting on his bed, his fists still clenched, his hair in his eyes.

"Ben, what's wrong? You like Trace."

He looked at his mother with disgust and then turned and stared at the wall.

She sat down beside him and tried to take his hand, but he pulled away, crossed his arms, and moved to the far corner of the bed.

"I'm sorry you saw us kissing, but I don't understand why you're so mad."

"I hate him, that's all."

"I know that's not true." She sat quietly for a few moments. "What's really bothering you?"

Ben's gaze connected with hers, and then he stared at the floor. "I hate him. He's gonna be moving to his own ranch when he wins Abilene, and we won't have anybody again." Tears formed in Ben's eyes. He swiped at them and sniffed.

Beth's heart almost broke. How could she have been so obtuse and reckless? Of course Ben worried about losing people in his life. He'd spent so many years without a father. How else would he feel?

"Ben . . . it's . . . I . . ." What could she say? Her ten-year-old son was right. Trace would leave them after Abilene. He'd have his own ranch then. And if he didn't? Well, he'd compete even harder. Her heart stopped beating for a moment at the thought.

Her mouth went dry.

"You kissed him. You told me you loved Dad. You don't need Trace. We don't need him. When he goes to go Abilene, he might not come back. And after he moves, we'll never see him again."

A new fear rose in Ben's eyes and Beth's chest tightened.

"Ben, please . . ." Beth stopped. There was nothing else to say. Ben was right. Trace was going to be gone in a few days or a few weeks, and they'd be alone again—or he might not have a chance to come back.

Beth pressed her lips together and closed her eyes. The last week with Trace had been like a dream, and she hadn't been thinking straight. She'd forgotten she and Trace were wrong for each other and that she had a son to raise.

Trace had warned her so many times he didn't want any real connections, that she shouldn't make him out to be what he wasn't. In the last few days, he'd hadn't made any promises.

It had taken a ten-year-old boy to make her see the light. Trace was never going to give up rodeoing, and if she asked him to and he did, he'd be miserable. How could she let Trace come into their lives and take the chance of Ben losing someone again?

Of course, her son hadn't been old enough to know Ray, but he'd turned him into an idol and created his own kind of loss. She couldn't put Ben's feelings in danger again. What if they got close to Trace and lost him? Hadn't her son been through enough?

"Ben, we'll talk some more tomorrow. Why don't you go to sleep?"

He didn't bother to look at her as he crawled under his covers. Beth leaned down and kissed his forehead, then found her way out of his room.

She stood in the hallway for a long moment, knowing exactly what she had to do—and she had to do it now, before she changed her mind.

Beth opened the front door. Trace was staring out into the darkness.

"Everything all right?" he asked before she could speak.

Beth's throat tightened. A feeling of panic slid up her spine, coiled around her chest, and cut off her breath. How in the world was she going to tell Trace she couldn't see him anymore and that it was over between them?

She gulped in the moist night air and squared her shoulders. She had to end it now. It had been a mistake to become involved in the first place.

He crossed the porch and wrapped an arm around her shoulders.

Quickly she stepped back. "Don't, Trace."

Even in the dim porch light, Beth could see the hurt growing in Trace's eyes. "Is Ben really upset?"

"Yes, he is, and . . ." Beth's stomach twisted into a hard knot of hurt and trepidation. She crossed the porch to give herself more distance from him. With just his touch, her body was racing with need.

But how could she have been so stupid and

selfish? For the last week she'd given in to her silly feelings and forgotten about what was really important.

"I can't go on with this," she heard herself say.

Trace took a step toward her, concern painted in his eyes. "You're just upset about Ben."

Beth held up her hand and shook her head. "No, it's not just that." God, would she ever be able to forget Trace Barlow? She already knew the answer. "I made a mistake the other night when we—when I let you into my bed."

Her words brought sheer pain to his gaze. "A mistake?"

She nodded. This would be better. Soon Trace would be in Abilene and after that he'd forget her.

"Yes. I was lonely. It had been a long time since . . ."

His mouth formed a firm, grim line before he spoke. "Since you'd made love to a man?" He finished her thought in a flat voice.

She could see his hurt.

So their union had meant something to him, too.

Beth shook her head and closed her eyes. She couldn't let herself think with her heart instead of her head. She'd done that with Ray, and it had caused so much pain.

"Beth . . ."

She opened her eyes. "Trace, I'm making the best decision. I can't live like this," she blurted out. "You have to go to Abilene, and I need to take care of Ben. We don't belong together."

He was looking at her with deep concern, and it tore at her heart.

"That's crazy."

She wanted nothing more than to fall into his arms and kiss him again, tell him how afraid she was that she'd let herself love him and he'd be gone. Then she and Ben would have to suffer more hurt, more pain.

I have to make a clean break now.

"I don't want any part of you." She crossed her arms and hugged herself. "I was lonely. I hadn't been with a man in a long time. You figure it out."

Ending what had gone on between them was better. "Trace, it's over."

Without another word, she walked into the house and closed the door. Beth leaned against the smooth wood. Her heart slammed against her ribs and a lump the size of Texas formed in her throat. Yet she knew it was easier to lose Trace this way, before they both got in too deep.

"It's better this way," she whispered, and tears rolled down her cheeks.

Trace stayed on the porch even after Beth turned out the living room light. He leaned against the railing and stared out into the Texas night. Their love had risen up so fast. Now, in a few moments, it was over.

He turned his attention to Beth's house again. The light in her bedroom was on. She was probably taking off her clothes or lying where they had made love.

His fingers curled into a fist, and he held it down by his side.

The thought of not hearing Beth's voice or seeing her sweet smile again tore at his heart. He wouldn't dare think about not being able to help her, to listen when she had a problem, to love her.

She'd become the best part of his life.

Her bedroom light evaporated.

He studied the sky again. The night was cloudless, and the black velvet cover was scattered with pinpoints of light. Trace reminded himself that Beth's news a minute ago hadn't been a surprise.

No, he'd been expecting the woman to come to her senses any day. And tonight, with Ben's help, she had.

Silently, he moved off the porch and headed toward the barn. He had plenty to do before he left tomorrow for Abilene. Halfway across the field, Trace turned to look back at the ranch house.

In the darkness, he could barely see the white clapboard, the windows, or the porch. An urge to go back overwhelmed him for a moment.

Then he remembered Beth's house was a real home. She'd made sure of that. And he knew another thing, too: He didn't belong there. He'd only been let inside for a little while, and now that time was over. He needed to forget about Beth Morris and her beautiful blue eyes, her laugh, and her goodness.

Beth needed a man who could help her keep a home for Ben, a man who knew how to commit to a family—someone who would stick. He wasn't that guy.

Tonight, Beth had been smart enough to realize it. She was right, and he was going to honor her wishes. She'd had enough trouble, and he wasn't going to cause her more pain.

Trace started for the barn again.

He had to get ready for Abilene. That rodeo was his one big chance to win his ranch back. But what if Beth needed him to talk to Ben?

Trace shook his head. He couldn't let himself worry about any of that now. Abilene was going to bring him his dreams, and he wasn't going to miss out.

Getting himself pumped up and winning the competition was the only thing that should matter to him now. Abilene would help him to forget what had happened between him and Beth in the last few weeks.

He'd buried himself for so many years in one rodeo or another. He'd just do it again.

Beth hung up the phone and looked at her son. They'd been standing in the kitchen arguing about whether Ben should have another piece of chocolate cake when the phone rang.

"You won!" Beth shouted.

"What?" Ben stared at his mother.

Beth crossed the kitchen and hugged her son as hard as she could. "You won the contest."

"What contest?" Ben's eyebrows knitted.

Beth took a step back and smiled. "Honey, the Fort Worth Western Art Contest. Your painting won the grand prize."

"It did? But it couldn't." Surprise etched Ben's face. "How the heck did that happen?"

"Ben, you're too modest. Of course you won. You're more talented than you allow yourself to believe."

"No, Mom. I'm not talking about that." Ben shook his head. "I didn't enter my poster. I couldn't have won."

Beth looked at the notepad she was still holding in her hand. With all the disruption and arguing in the last twenty-four hours, she'd forgotten to tell Ben that Trace had entered his poster in the contest.

"There's no mistake. Trace mailed it to the contest. You won, Ben. They're going to reproduce your painting, and it's going to be at every rodeo for a year. Isn't it wonderful?"

Ben scratched his head and then grinned. "Yeah, it's great. Maybe I can be a western artist like I want to be. This kind of proves it, doesn't it? I don't have to be a bull rider to be a part of rodeo."

Beth nodded, her heart almost bursting. "Honey, I'm so proud of you."

"That was pretty nice of Trace to mail my poster."

"He knew you'd win. He said so when he brought me the receipt."

"He *said* that?" Ben's eyes grew wider.

"Yes, he really believes in you." Beth pulled out a kitchen chair and sat. For the last two nights, she'd slept only a few hours. When she had managed to fall asleep, she dreamed of Trace. Would she ever again have a peaceful night's rest?

She doubted it. She was sure Trace Barlow would haunt her dreams forever.

"Can I have some cake now?" Ben asked for the fifth time.

Beth laughed. With the news, her mood had softened. "Sure. Cut me a piece, too, honey. We'll make it a real celebration and ruin our dinner. You're going to be famous someday for your artwork, Ben. I just know it."

"Yeah, I'm gonna be the best western artist this state has ever seen," Ben threw over his shoulder as he cut two huge pieces of cake. He brought them to the table, dropping crumbs along the way. "I'm gonna be better than that guy Trace told me about, the guy with all the statues. I'm gonna be king of the art world."

"Congratulations, honey." Beth picked up her fork and clinked it against Ben's.

He giggled and touched her fork again. "This is a real party. Too bad Trace isn't here. He'd have something to celebrate, too. He was the one who gave me the idea in the first place. He's a great guy, Mom. I like him so much."

Beth heard her son's words over the pounding of her heart.

I like him, too.

More than that, she loved Trace with all her heart. In the last two days since Ben had caught them kissing on the porch, she'd thought about him at least a thousand times.

With all he'd done for them, Beth knew it would be a long time before she would spend a day not thinking about the man.

Beth shook her head and told herself not seeing him was for the best. He wasn't going to give up the rodeo.

"You look funny, Mom. You OK?"

Beth nodded and tried to smile. "I'm fine, honey. I'm so happy about your winning the art contest."

"Trace left for the rodeo yesterday. If he wins, do you think he'll come back here?"

Her heart thudded into her throat. Ben always had so many questions.

"Of course he'll be back. His cattle are still on our land, and his belongings are in the barn. He'll have to come back and collect everything." Beth's chest tightened and her throat began to ache.

Trace out of their lives forever—it was hard to imagine. Her chest tightened more and her mouth grew dry. She shook her head. But she had to think of Ben and their life together. Putting her son first was the only thing to do.

Ben put his fork down. "I was just worried because he might not want to be my friend anymore after what I said the other night, the way I acted . . . like I was mad or something." Ben's voice broke and he stared at the table, his index finger drawing an invisible figure eight.

Confusion washed over Beth. She didn't want Ben to think Trace wasn't going to stay because of him. "The other night you were upset, that's true. But Trace knew that. I know he won't hold it against you."

Ben looked into Beth's eyes, his own filled with a deep sadness. "I miss him, Mom. I didn't mean what I said. But I get afraid when I think of Trace not coming back or being hurt in a rodeo."

"I know, honey. But Trace isn't leaving because of you." She missed the man so much her chest hurt every time she thought about him.

"I said some pretty mean things."

Beth reached for his hand and stroked his fingers. "Honey, he has to move to his own place sometime. But his moving back to his own place doesn't have anything to do with what you said. Nothing at all."

"If he leaves it's because of what I said. I know it."

She had to level with Ben. She couldn't let him think Trace would leave Oak Creek because of his actions.

"Ben, he's going to leave because we . . . well,

we were getting involved, and that's not good. It has nothing to do with what you said, or did, or anything. It's better he goes back to his own ranch."

Ben shook his head and then looked at his mother. His sad eyes, the blue of an early morning sky, almost broke her heart.

"The other night when I came out on the porch, I got mad because I thought about not having a dad. It made me feel afraid. But I'm not gonna be like that. I'd sure hate to hurt Trace's feelings again 'cause I was scared."

Beth patted her son's hand.

"Don't you miss him, Mom?"

She nodded. She wondered if she'd ever get over the heartbreak of losing the man she truly loved. But she had to fight her feelings.

Beth brushed at the tears welling in her eyes. "I'm sure Trace won't be mad at you. You can still be friends."

Ben smiled. "He'll come back and we can have another celebration!" He picked up his fork and clinked it against Beth's plate. "Come on, Mom, this is a party! Let's celebrate the fact I'm gonna be one famous artist dude!"

An hour later Beth stood on the porch looking at the Oak Creek barn.

Trace was at the rodeo by now.

Rodeos were so dangerous. Anyone, even a man like Trace, could be hurt in a matter of seconds in any one of the competitions.

Beth filled her lungs with the night air and

thought about all the hours she'd spent waiting for Ray. Many of them had been around a dusty rodeo arena with the noise and excitement. But how many nights had she spent just like this one, waiting and wondering if Ray would come home in one piece?

She'd spent other nights waiting for Ray when there weren't any rodeos, nights when her young husband stayed out—nights when she knew he wasn't alone and wouldn't be home until early morning.

Beth opened her eyes and stared at the night sky. Trace was older and different from Ray. He'd helped her survive the last few weeks, and he'd been a lifesaver with Ben.

Her heart swelled with more love.

He'd entered Ben in the contest with so little said she'd almost forgotten about it. He didn't brag about things or want any thanks at all.

Beth crossed her arms and leaned against the railing. Why couldn't she just let herself love Trace?

I felt scared!

Her son's words pounded through her thoughts.

She hadn't told Ben, but she was afraid, too. Beth uncrossed her arms and rubbed her temples. Her head was throbbing. She blinked back her tears.

She loved Trace, and he loved her.

But would he still love her after what she'd said? How could he?

Why did love have to be so scary? If she let herself care for Trace the way she wanted to, she doubted she'd ever get over her fear of losing him.

How could she put Trace through her worries? She'd smother him with all her fears.

Beth took a deep breath and knew she'd rather lose Trace now than when their love was deep and strong from years of being together, or when he got tired of her fretting.

How could she lose him and go on after they'd formed a history together?

Beth heard herself sob. Her life had been filled with broken dreams, sand castles she'd built and then seen dashed to nothing.

She couldn't let herself love Trace and take the chance of getting hurt again. She wouldn't survive—but she had to, for Ben. She was all he had.

Beth crossed her arms again and straightened her spine. She had to stick with her decision. She'd told Trace good-bye. No matter how much she loved him, their lives had to stay apart.

SIXTEEN

Beth sat on the couch and poured her afternoon diet soda into the icy glass. She was exhausted. She'd stayed out on the porch much too late last night, and when she'd tried to go to sleep, she'd tossed and turned most of the night.

"M-o-o-o-m!" Ben galloped through the front door, his hair flying, his lips pulled into a big grin. He cut across the living room toward the kitchen.

"I'm right here, honey. You don't have to yell."

Ben skidded to a stop in the middle of the room and turned around. "I thought you were in the kitchen." He closed the space between them, plopped on the couch and picked up the remote to the TV.

The set blared on, and Ben clicked it at a rapid pace.

"Ben, turn it down and stay on one station for at least a minute. How can you tell what's on TV when you click it every two seconds?"

"Aw, geez, I can hardly hear it now, and this all stinks. Why are there so many talk shows?" He pressed the volume button down, but clicked the station button again. "The news, yuck!"

A rodeo contestant has been killed at the Abilene—

Ben clicked to cartoons and turned up the volume.

Stunned, Beth sat very still for a moment, then faced her son. "Turn it back to the news for a minute." To her surprise, Ben clicked it back without an argument.

Until further notification of his family, the authorities are not releasing a name. Once again, a contestant has been killed at the Abilene Rodeo. Live report at six.

Beth's heart beat into her throat. For a moment, she wondered if she'd be able to breathe again.

Someone killed in Abilene.

The words hammered and tumbled through her mind.

What if it's Trace?

Beth closed her eyes.

God, please don't let it be Trace.

"Mom."

Beth opened her eyes and stared at her son. He sat on the couch, his eyes wide, his mouth gaping.

She wasn't even sure how long he'd been calling to her. Beth reached over and turned the TV to the cartoons.

"Mom, do you think it's Trace?"

Beth pressed her lips together and shook her head. She wasn't sure about anything any more. What if it was Trace? She couldn't let herself think about that now. Ben was upset, and she had to be strong for him.

Drawing in a deep breath, she told herself again to be calm for Ben's sake. "Honey, Trace doesn't ride bulls anymore, so it's probably not him."

"But they didn't say it was a bull rider. Accidents happen with ropers, too."

"Yes, but that's not the most dangerous competition. The odds of its being Trace are really low."

Ben nodded, yet turned the TV off and stood. "I'm going down to the barn. Will you call me if you hear anything?"

"I will." Every part of her body was numb with fear and apprehension. She'd told Ben not to worry, yet she knew all rodeo events held some danger.

A moment later she found herself outside, walking toward the barn. Beth stopped in the middle of the field and stared up at the blue sky.

What if it was Trace who was killed?

Beth put her hands over her face. Trace had done so much for her and her son, and now he might be gone.

She might have lost him forever.

Love for Trace pulsed through her body. She'd ended their union in fear and confusion, thinking she could forget him someday, but loving

Trace with all her heart wasn't a decision she'd ever be able to change.

Beth couldn't move out of the field as tears ran down her face. Trace had understood she needed help with Ben when she hadn't known it herself. She was sure he loved her with all his heart. And he loved her son, too.

What if Trace had gone to Abilene believing she didn't love him, didn't care about him?

Hurt raced through her body. If the cowboy was Trace, she'd never forgive herself. She turned and looked at the barn, stared at Trace's window.

And suddenly Beth knew her love for him was stronger than her fear of losing him.

She wiped the tears away. This was no time to cry. She stared at the barn again. Maybe the man killed wasn't Trace. He had to be alive. Something deep inside her told Beth she'd rather have days with fear and Trace than not have him at all.

Beth closed her eyes. If Trace was all right, she was going to tell him she loved him and didn't want to be without him. And if he still loved her—well, she wasn't sure what would happen.

She'd just love Trace with all her heart and take what came along.

"Hey, Barlow, how you doing?"

Trace lifted his chin and nodded to the cowboy who'd slapped him on the back and then leaned against the bar beside him.

He glanced down the bar. The Roundup was filled with one form of rodeo rider or another, but most of the usually loud, excited cowboys stood silently drinking their beers.

He'd seen the accident—the man flung into the air, then landing on his head, his neck broken. Then he'd watched as the cowboy's family ran toward the arena, their eyes dazed and glassy.

The sight of two kids and a cowboy's wife running toward the arena had bothered him more than he'd thought possible, and he knew why. He pictured Beth and Ben running toward his body, their hearts in their throats.

Jeb Taylor. Gone.

Hell, he and Jeb were the same age and had been in most of the same rodeos all these years.

Trace wiped his hand across his tired eyes. Even with the excitement of his competition coming up, he could only think about Beth. The two days since he'd seen her felt like two years. What would she say about the accident? Trace imagined her blue eyes growing cloudy and her face full of worry.

"Hey, Trace, you're the favorite to win tomorrow. Everybody says so. No one else has a chance." Bob Jacobs still stood beside him and offered his hand.

"Thanks. I've been waiting a long time for this." He knew Bob was right. He'd checked out his competitors and the money—the win—was in the bag.

"Too bad about Taylor. He was chasing that big rodeo dream in the sky. Maybe he'll catch it now."

Trace nodded. Jeb Taylor had spent most of his life trying to win some rodeo competition, and now he was dead because of it. His family was going to be alone.

Just like Beth and Ben.

"What time's your event tomorrow?" Bob asked.

"Two."

Tomorrow.

There were always tomorrows—waiting for the gate to open and hoping your luck hadn't run out. Had Jeb been sitting in this same bar last night wondering if he had a chance of winning? Had he been sitting on the same bar stool thinking about his wife?

Trace looked down the bar. He'd waited all year for this rodeo. Now, the night before his event, he felt hollow and wondered what in the hell he was doing here.

He glanced toward Bob. "Ever ask yourself why we're still busting our brains and butts for a few dollars?"

Bob laughed and slapped him on the back. "In your case, it's not a few dollars. But sure, I think about it. The way I figure, we've made a pact with the devil. What the heck does my wife call it?"

The cowboy rubbed his chin and thought for a moment.

"Oh, yeah, one of those new-millennium, hyphenated words. We're commitment-oriented. We've dedicated our lives to busting our asses and our heads. She's always talking about commitment and how I've committed my life to the rodeo instead of my family."

Trace stared straight ahead.

He'd done the same thing for a lot of years. He was chasing a dream that didn't even exist anymore, and the accident today had shaken him up enough to realize it. Was the pipe dream worth giving up any more of his life?

Beth.

For the last two days he'd felt the need to talk to her, and now it was overwhelming him. He wanted to hear her sweet voice and see her face, kiss her lips again, and tell her how he felt about Taylor's death.

He needed to share so many things with her.

Days ago, Beth had said he was too hard on himself, and he hadn't had the good sense to believe her. He'd been pledging himself to the wrong darned thing for so long. If he didn't have this rodeo fire under his belt, maybe he could make a life with Beth. They could make a home together and help Ben grow up.

Trace looked around the bar.

Suddenly he realized he didn't need the rodeo anymore. He had new dreams on his horizons.

He loved Beth. They'd make new commitments together, build on the love between them.

His chest tightened.

But Beth had been serious when she told him she couldn't continue. What if she really didn't want to take a chance with him?

Trace faced the question. He knew for a fact Beth loved him. She wasn't the type to throw around words like love without meaning what she said. And the way she'd made love to him spoke volumes about how she felt.

A woman like Beth didn't give her body unless she gave her heart, too.

Trace stood.

"You going somewhere?" Bob asked.

"Yeah, I'm heading out, heading home."

"But what about your event tomorrow?"

Trace dug in his pocket for his pickup keys. "I'm going home to my family—where I belong."

Beth shifted her gaze to the road after she'd put the small suitcase in the trunk of her car. The next thing to do was to find Ben, then lock up the house and head for Abilene.

Last night after she'd heard it wasn't Trace, she'd tried to sleep but couldn't. Early this morning she'd made up her mind.

She had to see Trace, and going to Abilene was the only way. Her heart slammed against her ribs at the thought of seeing him in a few hours at the rodeo. Beth turned and leaned against the car. She'd promised herself she would fight her fears. What she'd experienced years ago was gone, and now she needed to start her and Ben's lives over—with Trace.

Her plans were all set. When she saw Trace, she'd explain how she felt, what she had thought about, and go from there. She'd tell Trace she was willing to be brave for him if he was willing to be part of their family.

Beth turned toward the barn and saw the black slash against the horizon before she heard the familiar engine. She blinked and told herself she was imagining things. But when the truck pulled into the long driveway leading up to the house, her breath caught in her throat.

It was Trace!

Suddenly the truck and horse trailer were close enough that she could see his black cowboy hat in the cab.

He'd come home!

She couldn't move.

God, it was so good to see him again.

He pulled up next to her car and hopped out of his truck, a smile on his face.

"Trace, it's you!" She crossed the drive and stood in front of him, her body trembling slightly. "You're back early."

"Yep. I decided to forget Abilene."

They were only a few feet apart, but to Beth it felt like miles. How she longed for Trace to take her in his arms and hold her. "You didn't compete?"

Trace shook his head as his lips pressed into a firm line. "I wanted to talk to you and help you with Ben. Forget the money. I'll get it some other way."

"Ben! He won the contest!"

Trace smiled. "I'm not surprised. He's good."

"And he's sorry about what he said."

"I know."

She stared at him for a moment, just enjoying him. "You didn't compete? Can we talk about that?" Beth couldn't believe Trace was standing right there staring at her. Even though it had only been two days since she'd seen him, it felt like years.

"Yeah, talk. It's one of the things I think we do best. Among others." He arched one dark brow and laughed.

Her body trembled and she swallowed hard. "We do a lot of things well together."

"True."

"You're not going to buy back your place right away? You won't be moving?"

"Nope. I'm hoping you won't throw me out. I left the rodeo early because I wanted to come back to see if you've changed your mind. There was an accident in Abilene, and it made me realize I'm getting too old to be hauling my butt around the circuit. I need to settle down."

Beth closed her eyes and digested his words. She felt her eyes begin to tear with sheer relief.

"Beth?"

His fingers wrapped around her upper arm

and he gently pulled her to him. When she was in his arms, she rested her head against his chest. He surrounded her and she felt the wonder of love.

"Trace, I thought you had been killed. I don't think I could have stood it if it had been you," she whispered, almost afraid to speak the words.

Trace stroked her hair gently, leaned down and kissed her forehead. "I thought about that, too. Made me realize what's really important."

"Important? What is important to you, Trace?"

"The accident made me see I've been committing myself to the wrong dream for too long. I'm quitting the circuit before I get hurt again. Let the younger guys take their chances and be rodeo heroes, have the glory. I never thought I could settle down, but now with you, I want to, Beth."

"Oh, Trace!"

"If you'll have me, we can make a life together."

Beth took a deep breath, enjoying Trace's warmth, his scent, his closeness.

"You aren't saying much."

She leaned back and smiled up at him. "Right before you drove up, I was packing my car so Ben and I could drive to Abilene to tell you something."

He smiled and nodded. "Something important?"

"That I love you, and I want to make a life with you, too. The other night"—she dipped her chin a moment to gain strength and then looked into his waiting, velvety gaze—"I wasn't being honest the other night when I told you our love-making didn't mean anything."

Trace pulled her closer. "I didn't believe you. Not for a minute."

Beth wrapped her arms around Trace's neck and hugged him hard. God, it felt so good to have him back in her arms.

"I'm not going to worry anymore about losing you. I'm just going to love you with all my heart. I'll support you in anything you want to do."

"Sounds like a good plan to me. But I'd like to add one more request," Trace said.

"And what would that be?" Beth's heart was bursting with happiness. Thank goodness they had each other. She raised up on tiptoes and placed a soft kiss on his mouth. Butterflies took flight and she hugged him harder. "Tell me what you want."

"I want to marry you. I want to help you raise Ben. And I want us to be a family. Will you marry me, Beth?"

He leaned down and kissed her lips, gently at first, and then more aggressively. Then he pulled back and looked deep into her gaze. "I love you, Beth. We belong together."

"Yes, Trace. I'll marry you—yes, a thousand times yes."

BOOK YOUR PLACE ON OUR WEBSITE AND MAKE THE READING CONNECTION!

We've created a customized website just for our very special readers, where you can get the inside scoop on everything that's going on with Zebra, Pinnacle and Kensington books.

When you come online, you'll have the exciting opportunity to:

- View covers of upcoming books
- Read sample chapters
- Learn about our future publishing schedule (listed by publication month *and author*)
- Find out when your favorite authors will be visiting a city near you
- Search for and order backlist books from our online catalog
- Check out author bios and background information
- Send e-mail to your favorite authors
- Meet the Kensington staff online
- Join us in weekly chats with authors, readers and other guests
- Get writing guidelines
- AND MUCH MORE!

**Visit our website at
http://www.zebrabooks.com**

Put a Little Romance in Your Life With
Fern Michaels

Put a Little Romance in Your Life With
Janelle Taylor